ARTCITY
A NOVEL

I0668268

JOHNNY VOCE

TWO STARS PUBLISHING HOUSE

G.K. Chesterton's definition of a novel:
"I merely say, therefore, that when I say 'novel,' I mean a fictitious narrative (almost invariably, but not necessarily, in prose) of which the essential is that the story is not told for the sake of its naked pointedness as an anecdote, or for the sake of the irrelevant landscapes and visions that can be caught up in it, but for the sake of some study of the difference between human beings."[1]

DEDICATION

For all those seeking the marriage of faith and reason.

Chapter One:
A Proem

Back then, everybody was shouting back and forth about change, but nobody had any clue how to fix a culture. When a culture gets contaminated, no amount of legislation or polls or statistics can ever fix it. When a culture needs direction, only the artists can regenerate it.

It was springtime when Vincent Fides, the peddler of dreams, stumbled through the countryside just outside Artcity. He was lost at the time, as no one knows the directions to Artcity, and while he had hoped to find the old city, he doubted he could. It was a quest for a lost treasure, exciting but unpromising. He had the usual salesman's outfit on, half a suit on him, the other half in his bag, his sleeves rolled up, tie and top button loosened, the traveling man traveling again. His tie was one of those typical diagonal stripe patterns, blue and green, the kind of tie that says, "I'm wearing a suit, aren't I?" He had his favorite fedora on, a dark brown to match his suit (well at least the pants that he was wearing of the suit). And on his shoulder, a thin bamboo cane with a bundle tied to it.

Vincent called this his dreambag, and it was pretty cool, because no one was ever quite sure how he fit all of his products in the little thing.

The terrain between the nearest towns and Artcity is quite varied. Within the past half hour, Vincent was somewhat puzzled crossing a desert (albeit a short one about a mile squared), a mountain, a plain, a plateau, and a pond. He thought to himself, 'What sort of a place has a desert, a mountain, a plain, a plateau, and a pond right next to each other?' Part of him wondered if such a wondrous terrain meant he just might be nearing his lost treasure. He marched on. A loud jungle, a smelly swamp, a dark cave, and finally an ocean. He didn't want to go all the way back through the dark cave, the smelly swamp, the loud jungle, the pond, the plateau, and the plain, the mountain and the desert, so he decided to walk on the beach for a while.

Vincent Fides, the peddler of dreams, walked and walked, watching the ocean, and wondering what a place called Artcity would look like. The beach was full of soft, white sand that tripped Vincent every once in a while when he got too sure of his steps. The cave he had come out of was one of many in a large plateau-like rock that trapped the beach to the ocean. Vincent thought to himself that the caves looked like the tall aisles of a grocery store, dark and long, separate worlds with only a coincidence of proximity. It seemed like days that he walked on that beach, but it was only one hundred and thirteen minutes before he noticed some notches at the entrance to a cave that looked like a ladder. Excited, he ran to the cave wall and started climbing.

As he tipped his head over the plateau, he saw a vast grassy plain that stretched for miles, and off, deep in the distance, the brightly colored skyline of Artcity. He knew instantly that it was Artcity, because he had never seen a red skyscraper before. 'Most skyscrapers are concrete and gray, maybe black, but never red. Henceforth, given the presence of a red skyscraper, that must be Artcity,' he reasoned. He was very intelligent indeed. He propped his elbow up on the plateau, then a knee, then his hip, and climbed up to the grassy plain to begin walking again. About halfway to the City, his philosophical reasoning was confirmed by an enormous blue sign, "Welcome to Artcity."

The moment he had finished reading the sign, he was startled as he heard a very loud concertina, the music seeming to be right next to him. He looked around, in every direction, but saw no one. He jumped again when a very loud voice chimed in,

"Open your eyes to see
  what no eye has seen!
Open your ears and hear
  what no ear has heard!
All has been readied for the mind of man
  who has the courage to believe!
All has been readied for the lover
  who surrenders to his cry-
Artcity is this way, and alive!"
He began to run.

As he was running, he never noticed a smiling, bearded, olive-skinned man appear sitting atop the sign, his legs and huge red shoes dangling over the side. He was wearing white pants and a white vest and a white shirt, with a solid red tie, accented by a boater hat with a shiny red ribbon, tilted on the back right of his skull. He was playing the concertina in a very slow, very intentional

6

way, as if each particular note were an individual place to be experienced. His name was Luce. Vincent didn't see him because he didn't know how to quite yet, but that would change soon enough. (You see, I don't enjoy not being seen, but I also can't force people either. I do love music in the morning time- there is nothing more romantic than a gentle, unobtrusive light.)

The concertina followed as Vincent Fides, the peddler of dreams, neared the outskirts of Artcity. His heart was racing, and his eyes were looking in every direction, like a booklover's first trip to the Strand. Over there is the skyscraper that's shaped like Rodin's 'Thinker,' lots of office space. Over there is the Arc d'Art. Over there is the Leaning Tower of Pizzas, our only fast food joint. Over there is the frozen pond where we ice-skate. Over there is the Great Wall of Cheese; it's not as big as the other Great Wall any more but that's because it was made of cheese.

Vincent was enthralled, looking around frantically with anticipation. Walking from street to street, he finally made his way into the heart of the City, the City Circle. As he turned the final corner to the Circle, he froze at the sight of a hundred foot fountain in the middle of the Circle, the font at which all Artcitizens gather daily to draw their life-giving drink, vino. What else for artists? We have a few water fountains, of course, but the unifying force of our City is celebration, of life, of love, of community, even of tragedy... in other words, very dry, very red wine, always in moderation of course.

Vincent plopped down on a park bench, watching the people fly about in all directions. It looked like New York, but people were smiling. Vincent was dazzled- Artcity was beyond his most outlandish of expectations. Vincent watched as a clown snuck very suspiciously into the

Circle, and while a child's mother was turned away speaking to someone, the clown began dancing for his adolescent audience. The child beamed back with glee, mimicking the clown's coiling. Vincent was still watching, though, when the mother turned back around, and her smile fell. She scolded the clown, her long finger shaking at the clown as she grabbed her child's hand and led him away. The clown's smile fell too, the paint with the skin, as his shoulders hunched over in disappointment. He put his hands in his pockets and slowly waddled away.

Vincent noticed the street peddlers, screaming out deals and pitches to all the passers-by. He watched them intently. 'This is my competition,' he thought. He could tell that the one with the bowler hat was peddling books, art books he imagined, or maybe blank books. The short guy with the long beard was peddling watches and jewelry. 'Must be fake,' he thought. He couldn't tell what the gal with the flapper dress was peddling; it looked like some sort of fish or shoe. The people passed by them all without much notice. Every once in a while, someone would stop and listen with a smile, probably just to tease the peddlers. Vincent thought, 'They've never met a salesman like me.' He tapped his dreambag with a smile.

Vincent began looking around to spy his first customer. He looked through his satchel to find something, then back to the people. He saw an older man with a limp walk up to the fountain, sit on the ledge, and take off his coat, wiping the sweat off his brow. Vincent thought anyone seemed as good as the next. The old man noticed as Vincent approached- he rolled his eyes and tried to do that most New Yorker of tactics, avoid eye contact. Vincent was too far though to turn back.

"Vincent Fides, the peddler of dreams. Ladies and gentlemen, for today only, I've got an authentic and gorgeous shoemaker figurine from an underwater village off the coast of Sicily!" Vincent beamed to the old man, pretending not to be speaking only to him.

The old man hung his head, and then reluctantly looked up to eye the little wooden figurine. As he saw the shoemaker, though, he chuckled a bit. He looked at Vincent, and without a word, pointed to a nearby shop window. Vincent followed his gaze and, to his distinct surprise, saw the very same figurine in the window display, along with a dozen or so varieties of shoemakers. Vincent was befuddled as he looked back to the old man, who promptly shooed him away with a gesture. The old man was wiping his brow again as Vincent walked over to the shop.

He was about to walk in when he realized the identical shoemaker was still in his hand- he nervously put the figurine back in his satchel, hiding it ashamedly. Leaving his dreambag just outside, he walked in the store, which was full of all sorts of statues and figurines, for a closer look at the shoemaker. He pulled it from the window display to examine it, and it was indeed identical. He turned it over, weighing it and looking at the close detail. On the bottom, Vincent found etched in the wood, "Made in Artcity." Vincent dropped the shoemaker, ran to his satchel outside, and grabbed up his own. He turned it over to see the bottom. "Made in Artcity." Nervously, Vincent dug through his satchel, turning every item over. "Made in Artcity." "Made in Artcity." A hat, a ring, a picture, a pen- everything, "Made in Artcity."

Vincent plopped down on the street curb. 'If my products are made here, however will I make a living for myself?' He looked around in a daze, suddenly tired of being excited, like someone who ate too much of a very good meal. On the other side of the Circle, he noticed a clown on a stage speaking into a megaphone. There was a small group of about fifty people standing around him listening, but everybody else buzzed around and by without paying him much notice. Vincent, intrigued at what a clown would have to say about anything, journeyed over to listen.

As Vincent neared the crowd, he noticed the clown speaker's baggy white clothes with huge classic ruffles. A single trademark tear marked the face of the speaker. The clown spoke loudly and clearly, "They have sacked our homes and pillaged our hearts. They have taken nearly everything from us. But they have not taken our hope. Then how do we respond? Is this not Artcity? Is this not where the greatest storytellers in the world live?" Many of the audience members nodded and whispered various agreements, while others laughed, sighed, and rolled their eyes.

The speaker went on after a pause. "Then let us rise up, brothers and sisters, and tell our story. We have been persecuted many times before- we have seen crisis and oblivion staring us in the face many times. And here we are. The crises have passed and we remained. Now our people are not welcome here anymore. How silly. We built this city, and now we are told that we are outsiders. We don't belong here? How dare they! Artcity will continue to fall without our help, so persecuted or not, we must rise up, brothers and sisters, to protect this city we love so much. Building the bridge between their world and ours will not be easy, though, precisely because they have far more dignity and beauty than they can see now, blinded by narcissism and hedonism. Then that is our mission. We must inspire the artist to discover beauty again...."

As Vincent was listening just then, he saw the most beautiful woman he had ever seen in his life walk out of a little shop on the Circle. He suddenly couldn't hear the clown-speaker talking anymore, his voice drowned out by the melodic sounds of my cadenced concertina. He watched her with his eyebrows raised so high that they might have been confused as a second hairline. He wandered slowly away from the clown-speaker's crowd, but careful not to move any closer to the young woman.

"Open those eyes to see
    what your eye has never seen!
Open your ears and hear
    what you've never heard before!
All has been readied-
    just open the door!"

She was wearing a light blue summer dress, the excess material seemingly dancing to the music, though there was little wind that morning. She had onyx-colored hair, that sort of shiny black, and the bluest eyes Vincent had ever seen, the only shade of blue recognizable from a hundred feet away- that sort of blue that is both bright and bottomless. And the most charming of attributes in contemporary Artcity, she wore melancholy mixed with a sprinkle of stubbornness in her expressions, or in her gestures, or in the way her shoulders drooped ever so slightly. Her appearance confirmed that she was modern woman, in all her glowing self-assurance and self-consciousness, her certainty and reluctance, her strength and timidity, those two inseparable and schizophrenic lungs that provide her breath. Yes, Woman is paradox, and the most beautiful and frustrating one that has ever existed.

While the girl was reaching through her shopping bags for something, a young man in glasses and a tightly tailored three-piece suit followed her out of the shop, smiling, running up to her with his arms outstretched. Vincent's head dropped, his eyes immediately falling to the ground... which was rather unfortunate because in doing so, he didn't see the young woman slap the young man's hands away. And just as Vincent depressively moped away from the young woman, she noticed him. She smiled gently, feeling sorry for such a handsome man looking so dreadfully depressed.

Vincent plopped down on a pile of trash bags, his head still hanging heavily downward. And just before he felt something sort of liquidy touch the back of his knee from inside the trash bags, he gently smiled to himself. He looked up at Artcity, the lost treasure found. He propped his chin up by his elbow, like the gargantuan 'Thinker' he saw on the journey in, and admired Artcity in all of her vibrancy.

Chapter Two: A Handshake

Rodin's Vincent sat there on his trash bags for over an hour, as still as a sculpture, except for his eyes which travelled the skyline, the people, the paintings that lined the sidewalks, the cars that looked like three-dimensional canvases, this one Michelangelo's Sistine Chapel, that one Dalí's Temptation of St. Anthony. 'That is the coolest thing I have ever seen in my life,' the thinker thought. Vincent had no desire to go anywhere else- he was sure that from this place in the world he could watch everything that mattered in humanity pass by, the truth, the goodness, and all the beauty we have ever imagined.

It was when the Dalí passed that he realized he wasn't alone on his trash bags. He didn't notice when a clown sat down next to him, a different trash bag, and was imitating the thinker pose with glee. The clown was concentrating on his pose as Vincent looked over at him. He wore Chaplin's tight jacket atop baggy patched pants and one shoe that looked twice a normal foot size- The other foot was in a cast. His pure white face looked like a Roman statue- that Carrara marble that made Rome famous and eternal. His eyes were marked in black, one with an x, the other with a cross. The clown, carefully trying to hold the pose, looked out the side of his eyes when he became conscious of Vincent's gaze. "What?" the clown asked dully.

"What are you doing?" Vincent said.

"What are *you* doin'?" came the reply.

Leaning back, Vincent mumbled, "My heart's broken."

Still maintaining the pose, the clown shrugged his shoulders, "My *art's* broken."

Vincent was confused by the response, but had already lost the ability to be surprised. "How does art break?" he asked with little interest.

The clown stood up, tapping the cast on his left foot with a cane. "Six weeks without dancing- it's like Lent... Name's Domino." The clown reached out his hand, and Vincent reluctantly took it. Domino shook it vigorously.

"Vincent Fides, the peddler of dreams."

"Ooo, a peddler? Can I hear a pitch?" Domino said excitedly.

"What?" Vincent asked dryly, as if he didn't hear the question.

"Please, please- Can I? Can I? Can I?"

"Not right now, Domino. I'm a little shaken up from my last customer," Vincent said.

Domino was obviously disappointed, but he was generous enough to nod sympathetically. It didn't take long for his interest to go elsewhere, though. "How does a heart break? I've never seen one before."

Vincent gestured over to the girl who had sat down on a park bench to admire her things. The young man had followed her, now sitting beside her with his arms outstretched. "That's how," he told Domino, and buried his head in his hands.

Domino watched with confusion as the girl slapped the arms away again. Domino, thinking he understood now, looked to Vincent with his arms outstretched. Vincent, of course, slapped them away, which is what the clown expected. As Vincent looked up, Domino's fists were clinched and his face looked concentrated and constipated. "What are you doing?" Vincent asked.

"Waiting for my heart to break. Does it happen right away?"

Vincent was still watching the girl, so he barely heard Domino's response. The clown shrugged, sure he could figure it out himself. As Domino was concentrating, Vincent imagined what it would be like to live in this crazy cartoon world. He wondered if the girl that he couldn't stop watching had a shred of normality or simplicity to her. Maybe she was one of those crazy, pretentious artist types, the type that scribbles a line on a page and stares at it for hours on end, thinking it's the most wonderful piece of art that ever existed. He smiled at the lunacy of it, though, and thought, 'No way, not her. She's the sophisticated type. Only high art for her- she probably hates the crazy artists more than I do.'

As the thought of pretentious artists crossed his mind again, he noticed Domino beside him, who was counting with his fingers, and biting his tongue with pressed and confused eyebrows. He thought he would save the poor clown.

"I didn't mean the process of throwing your arms out to someone," Vincent informed Domino. "I was speaking of unrequited love."

"Oh!" came the clown's revelation. "Courtly love! Of course, I knew that."

Domino immediately changed his whole demeanor, beginning to sway his head tragically as if to some great overture at the end of Romeo & Juliet.

Vincent rolled his eyes at the sudden melodrama surrounding him. "It can't be forced," Vincent told him. "You don't have to be blue if you don't want to. I have to, not you."

Domino barreled back angrily, "You don't have to rhyme at me, sir. I'm simply being playful!"

Vincent was stunned at the mood swing. He had never seen an angry clown before, and he finally understood why so many people in the world are afraid of clowns.

Domino went on to chastise Vincent sarcastically. "Adieu, wing screw, for such speech is imbued with the blue dew of toxins that pursue and subdue any listener into a taboo long deceased with truth accrued for misused hues of misconstrued canoes and tattoos full of two glues that pierce through the shampoo and infect any listener anew with rhyming like a blue fool..." Domino added with a finger raised, "Near rhyme."

Vincent defended himself, "I didn't mean any offense. I'm sorry."

Realizing he had gone too far, Domino apologized and tried to calm himself down. "It's okay, of course. I just didn't see a need for rhyming is all. It's no big deal, though. I forgive you."

Too frightened to enquire further, Vincent simply said, "Thank you. I am sorry."

Trying to be playful again, Domino changed the subject, "I saw you listening to Federico. Are you a clown sympathizer? Obviously, right? Since you're talking to me and all?"

Still on unsure ground, Vincent said unsurely, "Yes, I suppose I am. He seemed very intelligent. Is he an important man around here?"

"Oh, yes. Federico is a brilliant artist whose head is only exceeded by his heart. He's an accomplished pianist- well, I consider him 'accomplished'- And the leader of the Universal Movement."

Vincent said, "Is that some kind of science club?"

Domino went on, "No, no, universal as in timeless, boundless. Something that is universal cannot be fixed or contained in any way. Human achievement in this world has been extraordinary- We have come to understand so much about the universe around us, about ourselves, and about the Creator of us all. These are timeless truths, universal truths, that aren't contained in a building or a city or a nation or a century- these truths apply to all times and all peoples in all lands. Hence we call it the Universal Movement."

Vincent's Emersonian American conscience set in the moment he heard somebody had a truth he didn't have. "But can't people figure it out for themselves? Why do we need other people to tell us what the truth is? We have brains- we can figure it out ourselves." Vincent, like many Americans, found Emerson's essay on "Self-Reliance" far more interesting than the Declaration of Independence (all that Creator talk gets pretty inconvenient).

Domino had read Emerson's essays, too, so he smiled at Vincent's endorsement of a personal and therefore relative interpretation. "Contrary to popular belief, and common misrepresentation by our enemies, we are not adverse at all to the extensive use of our human reason. They know what we say of faith, but never listen to what we say of reason. Faith and reason are the two wings that make man fly, and you cannot fly with one wing- you need both.[2] Faith and reason could never contradict each other- quite the opposite. They support each other- they complement each other. Growth is the product of faith and reason, and it cannot be had without them."

Vincent objected, though. "But to say that is to say a man without faith can't grow, because you need both. Or a man with only faith and no reason can't grow. Human reason shows us that that's false."

Domino loved the challenge. "Ah, but what is growth, Mr. Fides? Growth is both the shedding of something and the taking on of something new, even if only to shed the belief that the present state is okay and doesn't need growth. Therefore, something is being lost and something is being gained. And that very process requires both faith and reason: faith in becoming something you've never been before, even if you have a 'reason' why."

Vincent asked, "What would the people who don't agree with you say? I mean, the clown speaker- Federico was it? Who are his enemies?"

Domino was glad the foreigner showed such interest. "Ah, the Age of Delightenment. They won't even call us Universals. They call us 'The Magic Movement.'"

"Magic?"

Domino looked heartbroken. "Yes, they reduce our faith, the belief in the unknown, to mere magic, to unfounded expectations and simple illusion. They think the path to a better world is getting rid of beliefs, or at least compartmentalizing those beliefs. You can be a Universal on Sunday, but don't bring it to work with you. In that kind of society, our differences aren't being accepted- they're being ignored. For fear of the confrontation, they want us to hide who we actually are. What they propose is indeed a certain unity, but it is a unity around nihilism, a harmony of nothingness, where we don't think or act or say anything that might offend someone who might disagree. But that's not a unity even worth seeking.

"What we as Universals propose is a unity based on a true dignity and a respect and a love of human life. We believe that all of us can indeed find a common ground. And even while we continue to disagree and even present our diverse convictions to the whole world, we can evangelize only on the firm foundation of that common ground: the dignity of human life."

Vincent thought about where he came from. A lot was making sense to him now. It seemed that a lot of problems in Vincent's society were just as troublesome here in Artcity. Vincent hadn't thought about God in a very long time. It struck him as kind of stupid since he was a traveling salesman who made his living traveling all of God's beautiful creation. He felt sorry for himself- then he was a little angry at himself- then he was a little angry at Domino's enemies here. 'It must be their fault,' Vincent thought (excusing his own blame, of course, for he was not yet far advanced).

Vincent asked, "How do they get away with it?"

Domino shook his head. "When faith and reason get divorced, the whole family feels the pain of it. Where one is lacking, both are. But it comes down to freedom, Mr.

Fides. We all want what we think is best for ourselves, but we constantly overlook what is best for others during our pursuits. All of life's problems come from this extreme individualism that rejects the other's desires for the sake of our own. The devil said, 'I will not serve.' Our enemies are no different- they chase what they want, and belittle and battle anyone who stands as an obstacle to that freedom. They even kill in the name of freedom, and no matter how often we declare that killing is wrong, they simply dismiss us by saying we're just trying to push our beliefs on them, as if by their own definition, they weren't pushing their own beliefs on us."

Vincent felt something in the pit of his stomach, something hard and heavy, rigid and mobile. Realizing that Vincent, a foreigner in this place, was distressing the good clown, he abandoned the subject in silence. After a few moments, he started rooting around his dreambag to find something. Finally he found what he was after. "Look, I've got a cane in here that could reduce your limp by two months- It's from the laurel tree that Daphne turned herself into, fleeing from Apollo."

Domino was excited as Vincent switched into his upbeat pitching tone. "Oh, oh, the pitch! That was good, Mr. Fides. I'm impressed."

"So you'd love to buy the cane, right? I'll give you two for one since I like you so much."

"Thank you, Mr. Fides, but no thanks," Domino responded. "I've already got a cane."

"But I bet it's not filled with magic," Vincent pitched.

"It's not? The wizard on Main Street said it was!"

Vincent slumped back down in the trash bags. "I don't understand. You guys already have everything here. I can't compete."

"It's Artcity. We made everything," Domino said proudly.

"I'll be honest, Domino," Vincent confided, "I don't know if I can stay. I just don't think I can make a living here. I mean, what do I have to offer Artcity?"

"No, no, no, Mr. Fides," Domino encouraged, "you're not just any peddler. You're the peddler of dreams!"

Vincent looked down. "Well, what do you do, Domino?"

Domino smiled largely and pulled out a business card for Vincent to peruse.

Vincent read the oversized 5" X 7" business card. "Domino, clown, magician, guide, dancer, pianist, poet, soul mate finder, sculptor, songwriter-' You do all this, Domino?"

Domino snatched his business card back. "Well, I consider myself a songwriter."

"Wait, wait- What was that last one?" Vincent sat up.

"Sculptor? Sure, I can sculpt very well-"

"No, before that," Vincent said.

"Clown?"

Vincent paused a moment to collect himself, which always means of course that he was trying to endure someone that was trying his patience- it happens often in the sales world. "Did you say soul mate finder?"

"Oh, yes, of course. That's my specialty!"

"Of course it is," Vincent remarked. "How much?"

"How much what?" Domino was confused.

"Money- How much money for your service?"

"Money to find your soul mate? No way- No deal," Domino said, a little offended by the proposition.

"I have to give you something," Vincent offered. "Isn't there anything you need?"

"Oh, I doubt it. My Mamma always said, "Ya ne'er need more than whatcha got right herr." As Oedipal implications came to Domino's mind for some reason, he added nervously, "We're not materialists, you see."

Vincent fortunately had never heard of Oedipus. "Of course," Vincent said awkwardly. "A wish- Some huge, important wish you've always dreamt of, but never thought possible?"

There ensued a very, very, very long pause.

Finally, Domino had his revelation, "I always wanted to own a theatre!"

"Perfect. I'll help you get a- Wait a minute- why haven't you just started a theatre then?"

"Oh the bank won't give loans to clowns, not for anything," Domino said tragically.

"Clowns? Why clowns?"

"The last acceptable form of prejudice in our society," Domino explained. "They say that we're outsiders, because we like things the way they've always been."

"That's actually the opposite of an outsider. That's called a native," Vincent said very slowly.

"Yes I understand that, outsider. Thank you for your illumination," Domino mimicked Vincent's slowness. "Now why don't you go tell everybody who doesn't have paint on their face- you know, the people who think that way?"

"Why don't you guys just wash the paint off your faces? You do take showers around here, right?"

"You really aren't from around here. If we could wash it off, do you think I'd be standin' here starin' at you with a painted smile on my face? Does it look like I'm *trying* to smile?"

"Okay, so nobody likes clowns," Vincent reasoned. "You've always wanted a theatre but can't start one because banks won't give loans to clowns, not for anything. So all I really have to do is sweet-talk a banker, in exchange for your services in getting my soul mate. Does that about cover it?"

"Sounds right," Domino agreed.

"Okay, I want her," Vincent declared proudly while pointing at the girl.

"Anna? I don't know, Mr. Fides," Domino warned. "She's Mayor Ratio's daughter."

Vincent plopped back down on the trash bags, "The Mayor's daughter?"

Domino suddenly thought of owning his own theatre. He looked at Vincent who hung his head low. Afraid of losing his beloved theatre come true, Domino quickly asked, "So we have a deal, right?"

Vincent thought about all the trouble he could get into, chasing the Mayor's daughter around: Secret service, hectic schedules, towers guarded by dragons. Vincent smiled. "Yea, deal." And the two shook hands.

Chapter Three:
Appointments

High above the music and dancing of hectic life in Artcity, a solemn man stared out of his skyscraping window. The office behind him looked like any other office, except that instead of the usual white walls (fitting for a politician, no doubt), this man's walls were painted bright green, that shade of green that you could never find anywhere in nature except maybe on a rare tree frog in a rare rain forest.

The Mayor of Artcity gazed out of his high window, as if watching the parts of an intricate clock working in perfect economy. In this case, the man saw a clock that he himself built. The man could see the successful parts working fantastically. And he could see the loose parts, the parts he sacrificed in his decision-making for the success of other parts.

The Mayor regretted his mistakes and sacrifices. He was that rarer sort of politician, a good one, a man who truly cared for the people he represented and governed, caring much more for them than for, say, his political party, or his lobbyists, or his campaign manager. And so when he saw the certain failures that had lived so other failures could die, he felt something deep down in the core of his being- that dirtiest of words in an arrogant culture: regret.

He regretted those failures as any humble man would, and should. In fact, he truly loathed the mentality of people who claimed that they had no regrets. He had heard their tired excuses many times. 'I've learned from my mistakes.' 'My mistakes have made me who I am, and I love who I am.' 'That mentality,' he thought, 'must spring from what we call evil: to dismiss others' suffering for one's own pride.'

He thought to himself, 'I have failed you, Brother Tree or Sister Sky- I am indeed sorry.' But the Mayor also understood that regret was not a prison, a determined time in a cage to somehow make up for the suffering a criminal has caused others. No, regret must be a tool, an asset. If regret is not used, directed towards a purpose, then it serves for nothing and can from now on cease to be used in the English dictionary.

The Mayor understood that his regret could be, must be fuel to his own purpose to help and serve others. No amount of works or prayers could ever make up for the suffering he has caused, but regret is not a past-tense word- it is ordered to the future, ordered to its potential. It must be used not to make up for the past, but to forge a better tomorrow.

He thought of those arrogant people who couldn't admit a single regret and they angered him, not that sinful decision of wrath, but that healthy action called love. He thought, 'If you cannot acknowledge regret, how can you ever truly learn, truly grow?'

While the Mayor was meditating at the window, a congressman sat in an adjacent chair looking over his notes. There was nothing noticeable about his suit or tie, or face or hair or demeanor, except perhaps a rather large red mark on his right ear. He called this a birthmark to any inquisitors but the Mayor and a few others knew the truth: that this was in fact the last trace of his heritage. He was actually born a clown. And so he will represent in Artcity a common problem in the world today: a clown politician who is far more a politician than a clown. A man who gets his ideas and arguments from political parties and mass media outlets and scholarly journals and any other trendy and fashionable source of "information." And taking on these external arguments as his own, he has in recent years become embarrassed to be associated with that group of people that is so untrendy, so unfashionable, the clowns. For the sake of convenience, he has come to believe that being a clown is far more a matter of practice than identity, and so he has changed his identity, contrary though it may be to the identity he was born with.

And just as the Mayor was thinking of that arrogant punk ignorant of regret, the clown politician looked up from his leather notebooks and broke the silence, "I am concerned about the clowns, Mr. Mayor. They are developing as a City power."

For a split second, the Mayor was very sad that he had to leave his meditation for business affairs, but his leadership wouldn't allow him to dwell on it for long, in public, that is. He turned to the congressman, "The clowns, Johnson? They're Anthony's problem. I don't have time to keep everything from disrupting *his* peace."

Congressman Johnson went on, "A problem we need Anthony to solve, sir. We have pushed them too far. Federico has them united, ready to fight if they have to. The Corporation cannot deal with a group of clown artists upsetting the monopoly."

"Oligarchy," the Mayor corrected with a raised finger.

"Excuse me, sir?" Johnson was confused by encountering a conscience.

"You know, Johnson, you used to stand for something," the Mayor said as he sat down. "You used to take great pride in your role as a public servant. It used to mean something to you. Now you're just the hired gun of a political party, cynical and tribal, nothing more."

Congressman Johnson defended himself quickly. "Well, sir, in all truth and honesty, I *am* the hired gun of a political party. I defend the platform against the other party's false ideology, and enact our platform into American policy-making. That's my job, and I do still take it very seriously."

The Mayor folded his hands on his desk as an elementary school teacher might during class. "No, Johnson, you are a public servant. Your job is to represent the people's interests, not your political party's. Now the people's opinions may not always be informed, so we cannot simply change policy-making as often as public opinion changes, as fashionable as that might be. But you must have their best interests on the forefront of your mind and the blade of your tongue. Otherwise, how different would our extraordinary society be than the old military tribes that flourish whenever there is a lack of leadership?"

Congressman Johnson adjusted in his seat, suddenly uncomfortable. "But Mayor, this is the way things are. You're just a dreamer. You want some golden society where everything works perfectly, and who doesn't? But that's not reality. This is the system we have, so we have to work the system to get what we want."

"This is only the way things are because of people like you, Johnson. You don't stand for anything. You have no character, no integrity. You are a hired hack that will sink into obscurity the very moment the people realize that you can't deliver them what they deserve." The Mayor stood and slowly returned to his window. "You simply need to learn a new word for your vocabulary, you and all those hacks like you. That word is ethics. Just because you can do something doesn't mean you should. As a United States Congressman, you are going to freeload on the American taxpayer every year for the rest of your life with a ridiculous pension you yourselves voted to enact. Meanwhile our veterans flood hospitals and make next to nothing. Our elders can't even afford to stop working until they're 80 years old. Aren't you embarrassed? Aren't you ashamed? All the backroom deals and negotiations and campaign funding- the people see all of it. And with every single rumor of corruption, they lose more and more faith in us. They're why we're here, Congressman Johnson, not for some political organization that only exists in two places: on a piece of paper and in shallow minds."

Johnson laughed out loud. "Then what would you do, Mr. Mayor? A third party? Everyone's greatest dream come true, a third party at last! Yet every time a third party rises to diminutive power, their greatest triumph and worst failure is simply to steal votes from the nearest power party. They are self-defeating and-"

But the Mayor turned and interrupted him. "I don't want a third party, Johnson. I want you to do your job."

"I'm doing my job, sir," Johnson shot back. "And my job is to tell you that if the clowns rise up and depose Anthony as Ceo, and without your support, it is political suicide. You'll be voted out of office before you can even pronounce 'Machiavellian.'"

The Mayor knew how inane the argument of moral responsibility would be to a corrupted politician, too common in today's political climate, and he didn't feel like trying to teach calculus to a third grader. The Mayor sat down again. "Do you really think the clowns can take over the Corporation? Anthony would never allow that, to the point of criminal behavior I'm sure. So if you think the Corporation is so vital to our economic well-being, don't tell me when you catch him. Or better yet, throw him another bail-out: poor people's philanthropy for the rich, your brightest political idea yet."

"Sir, do we have to go through this every day? You are the Mayor of this great City. Some things need to be done that others wouldn't understand."

"You mean things that others wouldn't agree with," the Mayor corrected again.

Johnson said quickly, "He is betrothed to your daughter, sir. Maybe a little more interest in his well-being is in order?"

"Ah yes, the collateral of my own family."

Johnson took a deep breath to gather himself, and like a kid chasing a doctorate before the firing squad, he changed subjects. "All I am saying, Mr. Mayor, is that the people need to see you on the side of the victor. If Anthony can hold them back, then we should give him everything we have to be sure of it. And, if the clowns are really powerful enough to-"

"You'd have me side with the clowns?" The Mayor was shocked, but not offended.

"You're a politician, sir. I am not asking you to like them, even to represent them. What we have to do is show the people your control, your leadership. And, most importantly, and now, we have to show them whose side we are on."

The Mayor had had enough. "Look Johnson. Anthony may run the most powerful business in the City, but I'm not stupid enough to give him free rule *over* the City. The artists deserve a lot more than he's ever going to let them have- What's he care? It's business. He wants profit, not art. So if I've got to be stubborn, let Federico and the clowns put some pressure on the Corporation, just to make sure Anthony doesn't get too big for his britches, so be it. Federico hasn't done something crooked his whole life, and you know it."

Suddenly, the most beautiful girl that Vincent Fides had ever seen walked in the door.

The Mayor jumped. "Honey, you almost gave me a heart attack. I asked you from now on to knock when you stop by."

Dropping shopping bags on the davenport (for it was old enough to be called a davenport), Anna said, "The grease you eat is giving you a heart attack, Daddy, not me." She went over to give him a big hug. It was the first time the Mayor had smiled since he saw her last.

"Sir, we have a lot to get through," came the nervous interruption.

"Oh, am I interrupting?" Anna knew better than to care.

Johnson answered, "Well we were in the middle of trying to-"

"Then I won't be long- will you excuse us, Scottie?" Anna sat in a chair opposite her Dad's.

Scottie Johnson bit his lip at the sound, as if it were an insult to hear his Christian name- excuse me- his first name. As he was walking out, he bitterly mumbled, "I've told you not to call me that, Anna."

The Mayor sat in the chair next to Anna instead of the one behind his desk. "What can I do for you, honey? Today's pretty hectic for me."

"It's Anthony."

"Not again, Anna. We've been through this a thousand times." The Mayor didn't want to sit there any more- he wanted to be behind his desk, but he didn't move.

"I'm not marrying him, Dad- I don't know why you think that piece of paper matters to me."

"You are marrying him," the Mayor commanded. "We signed the papers two years ago. I've delayed it for as long as I can, but there's just nothing I can do."

"I don't love him," Anna contended.

"So you'll grow to. Love is a choice, not a feeling, sweetheart."

"Yes, and marriage is a covenant between two people before the Lord, to love and walk together, indeed to be united wholly to one another. Do you think Anthony cares about any of that?"

"You've been watching ACTV again?"

"Yes," Anna confessed. "A clown professor was talking about covenants and how God is actually a family Himself, and He offers a covenant to us so we can join the family that He is. Anthony doesn't want to be a part of that family- he rejects that family. He persecutes that family! A covenant is not a signed contract- it's so much more, Dad! So why should I care about what that piece of paper means to him if he won't respect what marriage means to me?"

"You're talking like a clown, Anna. Now they're nice stories, really. They're cool ways of seeing the world- No one celebrates or suffers as well as the clowns. But at the end of the day, Vespers or whatever they call it, they're just stories. And stories won't pay your bills or feed your children or provide a retirement package." The Mayor saw well the gaping hole in his logic but it had been a long day of decision-making, and he wasn't prepared to be challenged on big questions just now. As Anna was rebutting his foolish statements, the Mayor got out of his seat and started pacing. He wasn't even preparing his next line of argument. Instead he thought, 'I've got to get rid of ACTV.'

And so Anna went on explaining to him how the clowns' stories are no less real than their own lives, both nonfiction (Did ya catch that, reader?), and how the clowns' reality is actually older and relatable to every culture or time period whereas their own lives are lived in one of those caves by the beach, the tall aisles in the grocery store, dark and long, separate worlds with only a coincidence of proximity. The Mayor didn't listen much because he knew all this and didn't dislike the clowns or their stories in any way. They were simply the same thing that is at the source of most lies: inconvenient for his argument.

Anna finally realized her Dad had zoned out. "Dad- Dad- Are you even listening to me?"

"What? Yes, of course I am, sweetheart." The source of all other lies: inconvenient for his peace (the lack of war variety).

"Daddy, this is Artcity. Our marketing slogan is 'where fairytales come true.' A thousand street signs and billboards and pictures and paintings- everywhere you look in this city: 'Where fairytales come true.'"

"Oh, don't give me that, Anna. Fairytales are for clowns and kids, and you're neither. Grow up."

Anna only smiled gently, not the smile of a superstitious child that needed to grow up, of course, but the smile of an intelligent and good woman who knew her continuing of this conversation at the present moment would only hurt someone she loved very much. Women often think about things like that- they're far more compassionate than men, whose competitive urges advance until a victory is proclaimed, by acknowledged defeat or tears. The Mayor wouldn't want his daughter to cry, of course, but so were his efforts frustrated at winning any arguments with her.

During the pause, which the Mayor understood well, Anna decided on a new line of attack. She had of course used all of these debates for the past two years since he was made to sign that stupid piece of paper, but she couldn't stop bringing the same old arguments up.

"He follows me everywhere. I mean, with how much money he makes, you'd think he'd have something to do all day."

"He owns the Corporation," the Mayor said with a sense of obviousness.

"Exactly," came the reasonable reply.

"No, I mean, he owns it. It's not like he runs it or manages it or- What, you want him to sew t-shirts or construct tables all day? That's ridiculous."

How a wealthy man has nothing to do all day still made no sense to Anna, but she didn't feel like wasting any more time. She skipped the rest of her argument about how wealthy people have more responsibility than those with fewer resources, because she knew that most people these days couldn't understand that to those who are given more, more is required, simply because most people these days don't even believe in requirements. To save energy for the climax, she skipped to the subject matter that always melted her father's heart.

"What was it like when you first met Mamma?"

"Come on, Anna. Every time we argue about Anthony, you have to bring her up." The Mayor finally sat in the chair behind his desk, but he knew, contrary to what the psychologists will tell you, the dynamic of the relationship would not change at all. The psychologists obviously didn't know his daughter.

Anna provoked, "Do you miss her?"

Every single time the Mayor heard those words, and he heard them a hundred times in the past two years, they cut his heart in two- a sharp, piercing insult rushed through his veins to every cell of his body. But it all happened in a split second- emotions are quicker than intellect, but contrary to popular opinion, not stronger. After that split second, the Mayor realized that this was his daughter whom he loved more than anything or everything on earth, and he realized that this daughter of his was simply trying to get under his skin in order to weasel out of a life-long commitment that he simply hadn't figured out how to get her out of yet.

We could go on word for word in the argument, but all the usual complaints and defenses have been summarized well enough. Anna knew she hadn't won much ground, but it felt better to speak all of her anxieties and frustrations out loud. She knew her father wasn't particular to having to hear them, but she simply wanted to reiterate, on a weekly basis, that there was simply no way she would ever marry Anthony Ceo, no matter how much money or power or influence he thought he had.

After Anna left, the Mayor didn't notice himself walk back to the window, but there he was, as always, staring out at the City he governed. He knew Anna didn't want to hurt him by always bringing up her mother. He realized that women liked to talk about things, and it was probably good for their relationship that her mother was still such a big part of the family. She had died eight years ago, when Anna was in high school. There was a plague that swept through Artcity, or- what's it called where you come from?- a virus. A virus swept through Artcity, the peanut butter or the spinach- I don't remember which factory it was. Just a reminder of how fragile human life is. The police chief, Frank Petrarch, wrote about death and mortality all the time- the love of his life died in the same plague. Frank and the Mayor were good friends, but they never spoke about the largest thing they had in common: the death of their loved ones to peanut butter.

Just as the thought of Frank's Laura came to the Mayor, he noticed a foreigner walking down below. As a life-long Artcitizen, he knew everybody who lived here, maybe not their favorite colors or television shows, but he knew their faces. He saw that the clown with the broken leg was showing him around. He heard about the clown who had broken his leg dancing last week. He wondered if a dancer could be very good at dancing if he actually broke his leg, but he didn't want to judge or anything.

As the Mayor stared out his window in a gaze, there was a buzz coming from a box on his desk. The Mayor didn't hear it, though. It buzzed two or three more times before the Mayor realized. He walked over and pressed a button on the box, "Yea, Cindy?"

The box spoke, "Can Congressman Johnson return, sir?"

The Mayor remembered that he didn't have time to meditate, at least during the day. "Yea- Yes, of course, Cindy. Thank you."

Chapter Four:
The Tour

Forty floors beneath the Mayor's window, the proud peddler of dreams, Vincent Fides, stood with his hands on his hips and his leg up resting on his dreambag. He looked like a Greek monument, a demigod, a peddler.

Vincent had a way of projecting his voice that only actors and peddlers know how to do. The words sounded like normal tones, as if he were speaking something softly to an intimate friend just next to him, but those normal tones echoed off the trees and buildings and clouds. Everyone can hear a peddler.

"Ladies and gentlemen, the peddler of dreams has finally made it to Artcity. I come from faraway lands with their faraway treasures, the rarest of pro-ducts in the whole history of humanity!"

The people were baited. A crowd of a dozen and a half people crowded around him, trying to get a glimpse inside the dreambag. Domino was right in front facing Vincent, and held them back with his arms fully extended to both sides. If the curvature of the earth were slightly different, he would've looked like Atlas with the globe on his shoulders.

Vincent didn't waste any time. "Crowd around, ladies and gentlemen. Crowd around." He pulled a veiled item from the dream bag and dramatically whipped the veil off and held it up. "Here is lot number one, folks! This is the rarest kind of flower on earth, a dancing flower! You just put a little battery in the back here, and press this shiny red button!"

The whole crowd began laughing loudly. They pointed and howled. They shoved each other aside to get away from the crowd. And the crowd immediately dispersed.

"Ladies and gentlemen! Ladies and- Where are you going?"

Domino was there to console him, as they were the only ones left. "It's okay, Mr. Fides. We'll find a way."

Vincent sat down on the ground and sank his head low. This dramatic action was not in sadness, mind you- What peddler isn't confident? This action was the result of an immense and confusing frustration. There is nothing more confusing than a confident person facing their own mortality.

Domino saw the epic struggle taking place. "We need to talk about the City, Mr. Fides. There will be plenty of time to peddle."

Vincent needed the struggle to end. "Okay, Domino."

Domino's cheer returned in an instant. "Good! Let's get to the basics- Founded, 1801. Population, 550,021."

Just as Domino announced the population, a man looked up from his newspaper on a bench they were passing. "No, I heard the Browns got divorced this morning. Sorry."

"No way!" Domino was scandalized. "I hate to hear that... 'Til death do us part,'" he said sarcastically. "So unfortunate." He returned to the foreigner. "Population, 550,022. City song is-"

"It changes for divorce?" Vincent interrupted.

"Yea. Married people only count as one person, of course. Patron saint, Santa Lucia. The city bird is the Eagle; it used to be the Phoenix, but she died. She usually comes back, though. That large green building is the City building. It's where the Mayor-"

Vincent was growing impatient with the sightseeing tour, though. "I get it, Domino- It's all beautiful. But where's Anna? I didn't ask for a day of tourism."

"The City building. You know, where the Mayor works? The disapproving father? You need to understand the City if you're gonna have a chance around here, Mr. Fides."

Vincent reluctantly shrugged in agreement, though he was obviously not interested as Domino went on. "We use Gregory's calendar and the Universal dating, but the Romantic time system." It sounded like somebody trying to explain why the Mona Lisa was a great painting. He knew those kind of people existed, and they called themselves connoisseurs or something, but he didn't need someone to explain it all to him. He just wanted to experience it, to witness the painting, to witness *to* the painting.

"Our currency is the Cloud. It looks like a-"

Vincent heard this, though. "Ooh, let me: it looks like a cloud?"

"Well, yea." Domino was surprised that Vincent knew what it looked like. He reached in his pocket and pulled out a feathery bundle of disorganized One-Cloud bills, giving them to Vincent.

"They're wet," Vincent surmised.

"Yea, it's getting ready to rain."

Vincent chose not to respond to that one.

They walked on, Domino explaining everything he could think of until Vincent found an important question that had been bothering him since he arrived.

Vincent asked, "There's one thing I don't understand, Domino. Artcity is full of beautiful works of art that surely can be found nowhere else on earth. But sprinkled throughout the City, I've seen many restaurants and grocery stores and superstores that I've seen in every city I visit. With such an emphasis on art and artists, how did Artcity ever buy into the corporations?"

Domino looked down at the ground, ashamed. "I know what you mean, Mr. Fides. Many of us are downright ashamed of their presence. But the Corporation of Artcity has made many business deals with outside corporations, and brought them all here. It's just money. If you've only got ten products, and I've got a million, you need to make a hefty profit on each one just to pay your bills, whereas I could make millions more while charging a smaller price. They say they're for the poor, the everyday people, but they're only for themselves, only for profit. That's why, year after year, and decade after decade, products get cheaper and cheaper. Everything you buy breaks in a year, and you wonder why."

Vincent said, "But that makes me worry as a peddler. How can I sell anything here?"

Domino shrugged. "If I had the answer to that one, I'd be a rich man. But I don't care about money. I've got enough to eat and drink what I want. Money is only a resource for my art, for my theatre."

Vincent hung his head as they continued walking. While looking down, Vincent didn't notice as his foot touched a patch of grass just off the yellow sidewalk they were walking along. Immediately, and nearby, the Sage of Rustici Palace looked up from his work and over to the patch of grass that he felt move. The Sage gently smiled as he realized that Vincent Fides, the peddler of dreams, had finally made it to Artcity.

Meanwhile, Domino panicked. "Oh no! Now you've done it, Mr. Fides. Come on! We gotta get out of here!"

"What? What did I do?" Vincent wasn't sure if he was supposed to be panicked too.

Domino led Vincent along a fence. "That's Rustici Palace. It's where-"

"It's a Palace?" Vincent said in a slightly insulting tone, as if he had ever seen a palace before anyway.

"Please!" Domino was still frazzled. "I'm putting my life on the line for you, Mr. Fides. The least you can do is refrain from interrupting me!"

"Alright, alright. Settle down… I'm sorry." Vincent thought to himself, 'Okay, no rhyming, no interrupting.'

Domino took a deep breath (it's much healthier than pills). "That is Rustici Palace, where the Sage lives. Anyone who has a question goes to him. Anyone who needs advice goes to him. Anyone who-"

"-who's in love with a girl?" Vincent didn't notice that he interrupted again.

"Well, yes, but-" Domino tried to explain.

"Then let's go," Vincent interrupted again.

Domino twitched with frustration. Vincent could do nothing but stand there as Domino stared at Vincent with a mild look of lunatic rage. Finally, Domino spoke, "No, you cannot go today. You have to get an appointment. And he has to accept your appointment."

"What are you trying to say, Domino? Spit it out."

"You don't have an appointment!" Domino roared.

Vincent was suddenly very much afraid of clowns again. Domino continued with more patience. "Look, there are three people who matter in this world. Luce, the crazy guy with the concertina, up on all the rooftops." Domino mimicked the hand gesture of playing a concertina and, to Vincent's amazement, the sound of a playing concertina was heard (I might have had something to do with it, of course). Domino continued, "Most people say he's got more power than anyone in Artcity, but he just sings songs." (And mind yourself, reader, Domino said all this, not me.)

"The second is the Sage of Rustici Palace, who seems to know everything before it happens. But I've never seen him leave his little chair over there- he won't interfere with our choices or opportunities, so it's still kind of up to us to live out our lives."

"What's he doing hunched over?" Vincent felt like a freshman in college who had a good question to ask his teacher- he wanted to impress.

But Domino was further annoyed, as if Vincent hadn't heard a single thing he had said. "He's a shoe-shiner-That's what the appointments are for!"

"The third then's the Mayor?" Vincent changed subjects quickly.

"No," Domino went on. "The Mayor knows a ton about the City, and gets pretty much whatever he wants, but his power is only political, only policies, rules, and laws. The Mayor sends a guy to the Sage every day, and another guy gets paid just to follow Luce wherever he goes, listening to the songs." (It's true- He even claps after every song. Less than genuine compliments are quite annoying.)

"Then who is the third power?"

"Why Federico of course. The voice of the faithful. The teacher, the inspirer, the mark of unity that we all turn to for leadership."

Vincent was confused. "But you said he has a lot of enemies. A lot of people don't even listen to him."

Domino nodded regrettably. "It's true. Many people reject him as an authority. In fact, most people are afraid of authority altogether. Obedience has become one of the dirtiest words in the language, but without leaders, and subsequently without unity, there is only chaos, only anarchy. Order is necessary, and Federico provides that order, much to Anthony Ceo's chagrin."

"And Anthony is the head of the Corporation?"

Domino didn't notice as he led Vincent right into a booth set up against the fence. "Hey there, Domino." Domino cringed at the sound of one of his least favorite voices in the world.

Before even turning around, Domino forced politeness, "Hello, Ms. Summers."

"Showing the newcomer around town today?" asked the woman behind the booth.

"Oh yes, yes I am." An awkward pause followed while the woman and Vincent stared at each other, waiting for an introduction.

Domino realized they were waiting, of course, but he still refused. Being Italian, Domino knew that an introduction was as good as an endorsement, so he would have to violate his conscience in order to be polite and offer the introduction. He remained quiet instead.

After the woman's stubbornness wore off, she gave up. "Hello there. Since my friend Domino here…" (Domino cringed at the sound of the word 'friend')…

"won't introduce us, I will. I'm Ms. Jaded Summers, ACCLU lawyer. And you are?" She extended her hand.

"Vincent Fides, the peddler of dreams."

She picked up a business card off the table and offered it for Vincent's perusal.

"What's the ACCLU?" Vincent asked.

She was excited to answer, as if she were proud of her affiliation. "The Artcity Civil Liberties Union. We make sure our great Artcitizens get what they deserve."

Vincent was struck by the similarity to an organization from his own home. "The AC...CLU." As Vincent finally realized why his host had been so reluctant to offer an introduction, he studied the card out of mere procrastination. He knew already that he didn't want to get into a conversation with this woman, but he was already too far into the confrontation to avoid one. He decided the only way not to talk about her was to talk about himself. "Yes, I'm new here. Just arrived today. I mentioned I'm a peddler, right?"

"Well, we represent all professions, Mr. Fides," the woman said, failing to realize that he was not asking for representation.

Vincent didn't want to tell her what he thought she did, so he thought maybe he could simply ask her what she thought she did. "So what is it that you do exactly? Make sure the citizens get what they... deserve?"

Domino had had enough of the bouncing around. He said calmly, without an ounce of judgmental overtone, "She's a thief and a hypocrite. No offense, Ms. Summers."

"Oh, none taken, Domino," the woman said politely. Surprisingly to Vincent, she seemed as if she had just received a compliment.

Vincent decided playing dumb was the only option. "I don't understand. If you make sure everybody gets what they deserve, how could you be a thief and a hypocrite?"

"Well, Mr. Fides, that's simply a matter of perception. What we think constitutes justice for each person is our estimation of what each person deserves. Some people disagree with our opinion, like Domino here. For people who don't agree with our views, I'll admit, we cannot serve them very well."

"So you pretend to?" Vincent tried his best to act like he was still playing dumb.

"Pretend to... pretend to..." she wondered if she'd accept the word. "Yes, I suppose. We have to pretend to. But the Sage pretends to, the Mayor pretends to- hell, even your singing friend (gesturing upwards) pretends to serve."

Domino was offended. "That's not true."

"It's a matter of opinion, Domino. If you believe in magic and all those ancient stories, then the Sage is for you."

Vincent's dumb voice was wearing off. "So you happen to have a booth here, near the Palace, to make sure that his is not the only opinion available."

"We... the people of Artcity... happen to have a booth here, yes."

Just as she finished the last hiss of her 'yes,' a very loud, very old bell began ringing about one and a half seconds apart. Vincent had never heard the sound before. "What is that?"

The woman looked frustrated. "I hear that dang thing every day and nobody will tell me what it is."

Domino looked down at his watch: six o'clock. He knew what the bell was but wouldn't dare tell the woman.

He nervously looked at Vincent, "It's time to go. We've got a lot more to see."

The woman conceded, "I understand, Domino. Be sure to show him both sides of the City, yes?"

"Yes, yes of course, Ms. Summers. I wouldn't want to misrepresent the validity of your viewpoints or anything, like with an oligarchic control of various media that serve as the citizens' only point of reference about life, love, culture, and humanity."

The woman smiled sarcastically as the boys walked away from her table.

Guiding Vincent away, Domino leaned in. "There's just one thing she can't get through her thick skull."

"What?"

"This is still Christendom. And we're not leaving," Domino said. He felt like a hero for the Faith, as he explained to Vincent what the six o'clock bells were for.[3]

Domino went back to showing Vincent various idiosyncrasies about the Artcitizens in the area. The guy with the lawnmower played a mean trumpet. The girl with the flowers was actually a painter.

While still at the edge of the fence, they got close enough to the Sage to hear the violin. Domino explained that it was an obvious miracle, that there was no one playing the violin, that there was no recorder or phono-something that was sounding a violin. Nobody knew where it came from. The Sage wouldn't say. The big rumor is that it was the ghost of somebody really important, who knew that the Sage was telling the truth, and so he followed him wherever he went like a sort of herald or harbinger.

"But you said he never went anywhere," Vincent said.

"Well, I've never seen him anywhere else myself," Domino explained. "But I heard a story from Federico that he saw him once in Clown Town, and the violin was there with him."

"Clown Town? That's like, your guys' neighborhood, I suppose?"

"Indeed. They won't let clowns own property in Artcity anymore, so Clown Town is all we have. They abandoned our police station and fire station and water supply though, so now it's pretty run down. But it's still beautiful if you ask me. Maybe more beautiful." Domino got excited as he saw someone approach the gates of the Palace. "Ooh, look. That's Congressman Johnson there, the Mayor's former campaign manager and chief advisor."

"Who's in the chair now?" Vincent asked.

The entrancing sounds from the violin seemed to hover around the shoe-shine chair, as the Sage of Rustici Palace was at his usual, smiling, fast-paced rubbing down of some shining leather. Beneath the brim of his flat cap, only the Sage's gentle smile could be seen as he worked. The smile he wore was his favorite, the one that only the simple enjoyment of hard and calculated work can give you. He was a specialist. He could feel his way inside the shoes, not the physical inside, where the wearer's feet were, but the spiritual inside, that nameless, descriptionless something that made this pair, this inseparable and unified plural individual unique. He felt his way always. But he could talk while he worked.

"A's all tha time I got, Smith," the Sage rolled his neck slowly, cracking it before standing up. "You tell Anthony all I told ya."

The woman in a fine business suit looked at the Sage's work, but realized that she had no language for understanding if he did a good job or not. "You are going to tell me something positive someday."

"Of course, I will… when ya get out of business!" the Sage joked.

Smith unfortunately didn't get the joke at all, hearing only that she would never get good news. "I have much thinking to do. Same time tomorrow?" She had a daily time slot.

"Sure, sure- Hey! You think 'bout dat choice you gotta face- I's comin' up quick!"

The woman nodded with dipping eyebrows, biting her lip and looking down as she walked away. Congressman Johnson tried to nod at her as she left, but she didn't notice.

The Sage's large smile got larger as Johnson sat down. "Heya, Scottie! Wha's runnin'?"

"I told you not to call me Scottie any more, Sage."

"Oh, I forgot. So, wha' ya want?" The Sage bent down and went to work.

Johnson opened his notebook and took out a fancy pen that cost him more than the leather notebook. "We need to know the capabilities of the clowns."

The Sage chuckled. "Jus' as capable as you n' me, I s'pose."

Johnson nearly jumped out of the seat. "Really?!"

The Sage chuckled again at the foolishness of fearing something you don't understand. "Sit down, *Johnson*. You'll havta rephrase yer question ef ya want a betta answer, I'm guessin'."

Johnson worried over choosing the right question, as if trying to find a question that had the remote possibility of getting a better answer than the last question. He decided. "What is the future of the clowns?"

The Sage waved him off with his rags. "Clowns, clowns- 'A's all you e'er wanna talk about dese days. Lemme tell ya this, Johnson- li'l secret 'tween me, you, and the violin."

Johnson leaned in really close.

The Sage lowered his voice. "Mayor's gotta bigga dream thin clowns 'n corporations. 'N 'at dream? I's gon' come true."

Johnson was scribbling furiously in his leather notebook with his more expensive pen, trying to keep up word for word. The dialect was admittedly difficult for him to imitate, so he used proper English, or at least proper American. "What is this dream of his?"

The Sage laughed. "Aw, you gon' havta ass *him* 'at question. *You* work fer tha man."

Johnson was still writing. When he had finally finished, he said, "That is it? That is all I should tell him?"

The Sage stood up, done with the shine, admiring his work from different angles, tilting his head back and forth like a confused dog. "I don't know what else to tell ya, brother. Give it time."

Johnson wanted more, but he dared not ask for any clarifications. The Sage, though happy and cheerful, didn't have a lot of patience when it came to politicians.

As Congressman Johnson walked away, the Sage offered one last comfort. "Things are changin', Johnson. You be sure yer on tha right side, mkay?" Johnson looked concerned, or maybe disconcerted, but he was not comforted. The Sage glanced over at Vincent Fides, the peddler of dreams, who watched him with his clown guide. The Sage smiled gently, and went back to work.

Chapter Five:
Tomorrow

In an elegant room of various shades of blacks and whites, with no thing or object exhibiting the least bit of color except a roll of bright red carpeting standing in a corner, Anna brushed her teeth as her best friend and maid, Bambina, removed what seemed an endless supply of pillows from Anna's bed. Bambina was a Pierrot-type clown, blacks and whites (for that is what her job description entailed), with baggy clothes that were obviously made to fit her older, and much larger sister.

Bambina was trying to begin a conversation, as she had just entered this scene, but Anna was constantly running in and out of her bedroom to spit toothpaste bubbles in her bathroom sink. Bambina noticed the red carpet runner still neatly rolled in the corner, and said, "I see you haven't used the red carpet I got you for your birthday yet."

Anna shrugged. "Too much color."

Bambina rolled her eyes, looking around the colorless room. "Where have you been all night? I was beginning to worry," Bambina offered without much worry.

"Rehearsal," Anna said muffled through her toothpaste.

"You didn't tell me rehearsals were starting already," Bambina said over her shoulder as Anna ran out of the room again.

"Because of stupid Anthony," Anna called from the next room.

"Big secret as always?" Bambina asked.

"Eye kand teloo aeeing," Anna said through fresh toothpaste.

"Huh?" Bambina didn't catch it either.

"I said I kand tell you aeeing," Anna tried as she left the room again.

"I still can't-"

After spitting the toothpaste out, gurgling water (which made Bambina giggle), spitting the water out, wiping her mouth with a black towel, and reentering the room, Anna said triumphantly, "I can't tell you anything."

"Ah, that's stupid. You tell me everything. If you're not supposed to tell me anything, you're rather lousy at your responsibilities," Bambina said as she tossed the last pillow to the ground.

"He acts like he's got the secret to the universe in there." And then, in her very best deep, male register, "Not till opening night, people. Butts in the seats- I want butts in the seats." Anna's very best deep, male register made Bambina laugh out loud. But Anna continued, "He's just so annoying. And he wants me on his arm for every event that happens in the City. I'm just a trophy- one more cheap plastic trophy to show he owns something nobody else can."

"He wants a beautiful girl on his arm. I don't see anything wrong with that- It's good for a young man," Bambina said obviously.

"Beautiful? I don't like that word- I don't know what it means," Anna said solemnly.

"That's cuz you've never heard a man say it to you," Bambina said nostalgically.

"The word only works when men say it?" Anna asked with obvious doubts.

Bambina began, "Well you're free to go in the bathroom and call yourself that word all you want, but I don't think it'll make you too happy. But if a particular man says it to you, no matter how crazy that man is- No matter how not-beautiful you think you are- You'll believe him, and you'll love him for making you understand that word for the first time. You'll actually feel 'beautiful.' Whether or not you actually are, I don't know- my last name's not Webster, you see. But the point is, you won't care what anybody else says, what anybody else thinks. So long as you're still beautiful in that one man's eyes, nobody else matters in that way."

"Bambina!" Anna said excitedly. "You never told me you were in love before."

"I don't like talking about it," Bambina said quietly.

Anna realized that this was somehow a sore subject for Bambina, and though she was infinitely curious of what happened to Bambina's Beloved, her concern for her best friend prevented her from probing any further.

Bambina knew well the immeasurable generosity of her friend, and knowing that Anna would not ask her an unwelcome question, she offered in finality, "Someday you'll understand for yourself. It's not something I can explain very well."

While not necessarily wanting the attention back on herself, Anna said, "That's why I don't think it's too much to ask for a man that actually likes me, or loves me. Anthony doesn't even know me- he just knows I'm the Mayor's daughter. I don't even need the fairytale, no knights, no princes, just somebody who understands me."

"You're breaking all the stereotypes, Anna. Do please keep your voice down," Bambina teased.

"Oh yes, as the Mayor's little princess, I wouldn't want to offend anyone," Anna said with false diplomacy.

"I believe they call it being 'politically correct,' little missy," Bambina instructed.

"Well I call it being somebody else, because that's not who I am," Anna said proudly.

"I'm a clown- I know all about expectations."

"That's right," Anna realized. "And it's not like you actually want to eat children, or whatever Anthony tells everybody you guys do."

Bambina thought a moment with creased brows. "I happen to... *love* children!" She ran toward Anna.

"Oh, shut up." Anna slapped the approaching claws away from her. Sitting down, "I just- I know there's someone out there for me, and it's just not him."

"There's the princess," Bambina teased.

"Ugh, don't call me that!" Anna looked like she had just tasted a mushroom, and she thought mushrooms were the most disgusting of the earth's fungi.

Bambina tucked Anna into bed. "He's out there. He'll be perfect for you. Just wait and see." Bambina kissed her on the forehead. "Goodnight, sweetheart."

"Night, Bambina."

The gentle clown turned out the lights on her way out, and slowly closed the door behind her. After the door closed, Anna rolled over to face the bright moonglow penetrating her window. She thought it looked like a spotlight in the theatre, and it was painting her blue.

Now at the very moment when Bambina uttered the word 'perfect' a moment ago, Vincent Fides, the peddler of dreams, had tripped on a rock while walking along a nearby sidewalk, just in case the paradox of what women want and what men are isn't clear enough in itself. Vincent looked back on the sidewalk confusedly, but found no culprit to justify his tripping.

Domino was still explaining things to him. "I don't understand what's so hard to figure out, Mr. Fides."

"Domino, your money rains," Vincent said with a pained face.

"So?"

"Hey, whatever. I give up tryin' to understand you guys. It's a free country… It *is* a free country, right?"

"Of course," Domino said with only minor offense. After a moment of walking in silence, Domino stopped suddenly. "Well, here it is."

"Here what is? The witches' house?" Vincent said sarcastically.

"Witches only live in the suburbs," Domino said without sarcasm. "This is Anna's. I believe that's her window there."

"You're kidding! Finally, you're starting to pay off," Vincent rubbed his hands together. After a deep breath, he said, "Alright, let's go."

As Vincent took one full step towards the front door, Domino, realizing that Vincent was making his move now, jumped in front of him to stop him. "What? No. Not yet. We've got some talking to do first."

"Talking? That's all we've been doing. I *do* know how to approach a girl," Vincent said with confidence.

"Okay, then what would you say to her?" Domino asked.

"Huh?" Vincent was caught off guard.

"Words, Mr. Fides! What would you say?"

Vincent just stared at Domino.

Domino had an idea. He ripped two handfuls of grass from his feet and tossed them on his head. "Here," Domino offered. "Pretend I'm her."

Vincent bit his lip, thinking, 'There's no way he actually thinks-'

"Come on, Mr. Fides," Domino rushed.

"I'm not doing that, Domino," Vincent said clearly.

"But you need to-"

"I'm not... doing that, Domino," Vincent said even slower.

After an offended pause, Domino said, "Then what do you suggest?" Domino answered with the voice of an excited robot, "Hello, prettiest and most powerful girl in the City. Did you hear? I am your soul mate."

"Stop it. Shut up," Vincent was not amused.

"Will you at least sleep on it? Tomorrow. Tomorrow, I promise, you'll meet her. She can't exactly escape," Domino said, gesturing around the front lawn that had become their camp.

Vincent thought a moment. "Alright... But it's not cuz I don't know what to-"

"Goodnight, Mr. Fides," Domino said, already lying down.

Vincent sat down. "Night, Domino."

Vincent and Anna stared at the same moon, being painted the same shade of blue, for about twenty-five minutes before falling asleep.

CHAPTER SIX:
THE DOOR

The blues turned into inconsistent shades of orange and red in that transitional hour of ecstasy before sunrise. Vincent, Domino, Anna, Bambina, and most of Artcity slept as the world renewed her pallet. But the Mayor was already up, tying his tie for a second time, for the first time had been a third of an inch too long, while gazing out his bedroom window at the regenerating sky above him. He thought, 'The sun has probably risen a couple counties eastward- It won't be long to reach me.' He smiled at the thought of the curvature of the earth, glanced in the mirror to check his tie, though he knew it would be perfect because he never needs a third try anymore, and ran out the door.

As the Mayor's utterly unmentionable automobile roared from the garage, Vincent Fides, the peddler of dreams, began to blink. Vincent was in that transitional moment of ecstasy between dreams, when the really weird stuff happens because there is, in fact, a second dream being born from a most random first. He was trapped in the back seat of a race car (for he had once been from Indianapolis) on a somewhat elevated autobahn that seemed to sway ever so slightly in the wind at such a height in the cold dark blues, never purples, of the night sky. It occurred to Vincent that he would rather be driving this car, else he should fall victim to someone else's insanity, but the speed at which his driver raced seemed to serve as the only seatbelt Vincent needed, as it plastered his body longways along the backseat in a somewhat contorted but surprisingly comfortable fashion. He decided the time had come for his transitional act of ecstasy, so he began using the wind and the curvature of the earth- I mean, his face, to work up in the atmosphere of the vehicle to look out the side and at least see where it is he was or was going, but just as his eye was probably risen a couple counties eastward, "Vrrooomm!"

The Mayor vroomed his engine, confused at the clown and foreigner that he recognized from the day before being camped out in his front yard. He called a number on his mobile phone, and sped off for work.

Needless to say, Vincent Fides, the peddler of dreams, couldn't survive the loud vroom of the race car, or was it the Mayor's car? He didn't know, and forgot what woke him before he quite cared to make the attempt to remember the dream. He surveyed his surroundings. There was a split second, of course, when he was rather surprised to be sleeping in the front yard of a house that he could not recall ever seeing before, but once he realized where he was, a swarm of butterflies in race cars began speeding through his stomach.

Vincent sat up, slowly looking around, enjoying that peaceful state between sleep and full awareness. His calm was interrupted quickly though when he was startled, as the next-door neighbor's door whipped open, a can of bright orange paint flew out onto the porch, and the door slammed shut loudly, all in one fluid motion. Vincent was not necessarily surprised, just startled. He looked around at all the houses on the block, and noticed various colors of paint in the same pattern on all the porches. It didn't occur to him to wonder why. He then looked at Anna's porch, and thought that the red looked like a two-dimensional flame, plastered on the ground, and protruding from the door.

Vincent looked back at Domino, who was still snoring quite loudly, then looked up at the window Domino had proclaimed Anna's. He began thinking of how they should meet. There was a wooden garden trellis from the ground to her second floor window. He thought he might have a peek, ala Romeo style. He snuck over to the house like a secret agent would, apparently unconscious of the fact that he had just slept in the woman's front yard, so all stealth had worn off by now. He took one heavy step onto the trellis, meaning to climb, and the light wood snapped loudly under his foot. He glimpsed back at Domino, who mumbled something incoherently before snoring loudly again.

Anna was in a gondola at the time, wondering why she was alone. She heard Vincent's loud snapping of the trellis wood, but to her the sound was an oar snapping off in shallow waters- she thought she was to blame and looked around to see if anyone noticed her clumsiness. She twitched awake in her bed, and stared at nothing in particular with wide eyes, not sure if she was still in a gondola or not.

Vincent, after a long sigh of relief, looked around the front lawn for an idea. His eyes eventually found his dreambag and the light in Anna's room came on over his shoulder, unbeknownst to him. With a slow-paced jog, Vincent approached his dreambag, opened her up, and began exploring the deepest corners of the satchel. Meanwhile, Anna quietly opened her window, and noticed Vincent's big butt flying in the air- she giggled a bit, but thought nothing of the people on her lawn. Vincent had found his grail and turned to face the front door, plopping a big, floppy postman's hat on his head proudly. The hat read in big block letters, 'POSTINO.'

Vincent immediately noticed that Anna's light was now on and window now open, so he began to panic. He looked around him, saw Domino sleeping (or rather heard him), and decided to wake his clown guide. "Domino." No response. "Domino," Vincent whispered a little louder. No response came. "Domino!" Vincent shouted in full voice, incognizant of his proximity obviously, for Anna jumped at the sound.

Domino awoke, which Vincent could tell only from the halted snoring since Domino did not open his eyes. Instead, Domino reached under Vincent's legs and up his back with something. "Hey!" Vincent said, noticing the fake spider and pulling it off. But as Vincent was flicking the plastic spider to the ground, he didn't notice Domino's hand return, this time taking hold of an ankle, and tripping him to fall flat on his face.

Vincent gathered himself, embarrassed that the half-conscious clown had outwitted him (but then again, there is little wit more powerful than that wit that wishes to continue sleeping). "She's awake, Domino!" No response. "I don't know what to do, okay?" But no response came. "Domino!"

"Alright, alright," Domino said in a tortured tone as he slowly began letting light in his eyelids, little by little, before sitting up with a loud yawn.

Vincent was near frantic, though trying to be patient.

"Well… what do I do?" Vincent asked quickly.

While Domino was stretching his neck, he calmly said, "Well, for starters, take that stupid hat off your head." Vincent took the postman's hat off, tossing it towards his dreambag. Domino continued stretching, waiting a far longer pause than it took Vincent to carry out the first directive, so Vincent stood looking frantically back and forth between the window and Domino.

Finally, Domino continued, "Alright. Now you have to meet by accident- that's the way it works in these things."

"Okay. How?" Vincent responded.

Domino began, "Well, you could-" But Domino froze with high eyebrows as he saw Anna return to the window and look out. Vincent quickly followed his gaze without thinking about it, and the two connected eyes for the first time, both looking quite dumbfounded with no expression whatever. After one and a half seconds, which is a long time in such situations, Anna giggled and scurried away from the window.

Domino continued consolingly, "Well, that was one way of doing it."

"Domino?" Vincent asked in a daze. "What now?"

"Pull yourself together, Vincent. I thought you were a salesman," Domino encouraged.

"I'm nervous," Vincent said with uneven breaths.

Inside, Anna hastily brushed into Bambina's room. "Bambina," Anna called as she entered the room. "Bambina! Are you awake?"

With her eyes still closed and a small grin sweeping across her face, Bambina woke only to grab one of Anna's approaching legs and toss her over the bed.

"Bambina! Wake up! You're violent in the morning," Anna said as she stood up and brushed herself off.

Outside, Domino directed Vincent to puff up his chest, lift his chin high, and smile. Domino assessed his work, "Now, how do you feel?"

Through the slightly vibrating clinched teeth of a mechanical smile, Vincent said, "Surprisingly better."

"Now, go to the door," Domino directed.

"The door?"

"The door."

"And?"

"And knock!"

Vincent's face passed through nineteen different emotions as he approached the front door.

"Outside? Right now?" Bambina asked.

Anna began, "In the front yard. Oh, if you would have seen-"

"Stop it! Focus," Bambina interrupted.

"What? What do I do?" Anna began to panic at the thought of meeting the young man.

Bambina thought out loud, "Well, obviously you have to do the morning ritual first. You don't want it to go horribly, do you?"

"I know," Anna said through slightly vibrating clinched teeth, "but he's out there."

"Then do it quickly," Bambina directed. "Open and shut."

On the front porch, Vincent approached the front door, all nineteen emotions now on his face at once. Suddenly, determination won. He decisively raised his hand high in the air to knock, like the back swing of a golf club. But as his knuckles with forward momentum approached the wood of the door, the door whipped open, the beautiful Anna launched a can of bright red paint in his face, and the door slammed shut again, all in one fluid motion. Vincent's eyes being as open as they had ever been before did not lend well to the accident, as the intense burn of the paint boiling his eye juices made him fall to his knees.

After the door was shut, Anna's eyes were as open as they had ever been too, but with a paralyzing fear as if she had just seen a ghost. She shakily opened the door again, and asked the intruder rather quickly, "What do you want?"

Stunned, Vincent sounded like a computer-generated voice, "Um, hello, prettiest and most powerful girl in the City. Did you hear?"

But Vincent was drilled in the side of the head by a very large shoe. "Ow!" Vincent looked back at Domino who stood confidently in the front yard with two hands on his hips, but wearing only one of his two very large shoes. Anna continued quickly, "I'm not supposed to talk to clowns."

Pointing in the house, Vincent replied logically, "But I just saw a clown walk-"

"Oh that's Bambina," Anna interrupted.

After a pause when Vincent thought the girl would offer more, he tried to gather himself. "So? Wait- I'm not even a clown anyway- You just drenched me with paint- Why are you throwing paint out your front door?"

Anna shrugged. "It's good luck in the morning." Realizing that the stranger posed no threat, Anna calmed herself. She called for Bambina to bring him a towel, which

Bambina did quickly. As Vincent was wiping his face, Anna finally recognized him as the young man from before. "Then what can I do for- Oh! You're the-"

In a sudden burst of peddlerhood, Vincent held out his hand to her, "My name's Vincent Fides, the peddler of dreams. You must be the Anna I've heard so much about."

"Peddler of dreams?" Anna asked with a giggle as she firmly shook his hand.

"Oh, yes," Vincent said. "I can make all of your dreams come true for you if you want me to."

"Well, don't rhyme at me!" Anna said, suddenly offended.

"What's with the rhyming?" Vincent whispered to himself.

Gathering herself, realizing that the foreigner didn't mean any harm, she put on as much charm as she could muster. "I feel at a disadvantage. You seem to know more about me than I know about you."

"I saw you in the Circle," Vincent explained. "So I asked my friend about you."

"Why did you ask about me?" Anna asked, like many women ask questions that men have no intention of answering.

The very loud sound of a clown guide on the front lawn clearing his throat made Vincent jump a bit. Vincent remembered, and said suavely, "Hm. Is that a... May I?" Anna nodded, confused of what he was talking about. Vincent reached under Anna's arm and pulled a single stemmed white rose out from behind her back, and gave it to her.

"Oh, thank you," Anna said, covering her romantic shyness with sarcasm.

"My pleasure," Vincent said as he threw a wink towards Domino his maestro.

"You're- You're not from around here, are you," Anna said.

"Do I stick out so much?"

"Well, you didn't know about the paint," Anna reasoned.

"Ah, yes," Vincent said as he picked up the rather large shoe. "The good luck. Well, my guide has taught me a lot about your City here, but he *seems* to have left that one out." It was on the word 'seems' that Vincent launched the rather large shoe over his shoulder in the general direction of his clown guide. Domino ducked sharply but confidently, and the shoe missed.

There was indeed a lot that Domino had yet to tell Vincent, for some things are so important that they must be experienced rather than taught, and of course some things are so unimportant that they never require mentioning.

Anna looked down at the ground between the two so often that she didn't notice the shoe bit. She continued, "Where are you from then?"

"Oh I don't know," Vincent acted tough. "Here and there."

"You don't remember?" Anna thought the tough act was absurd but cute.

"I just wander around from town to town with my dreambag." Vincent was at full pitch.

"Dreambag?" Anna chuckled.

"Oh, yes," Vincent defended. "In this little bag holds a dream for every single person I meet. Dreamt satisfaction guaranteed."

"You have one for me?" Anna asked innocently.

"I must." Vincent smiled as she took the bait.

"Well- uh-..." Anna backed off. "What can I do for you anyway? Is it sales? You want to sell something? My Dad must have left for work already, and I'm afraid he won't be home till-"

"No, no," Vincent said confidently. "I just wanted to introduce myself. That's all."

"That's all?" Anna didn't believe him.

"Yea, for now anyway. I'm sure I'll be seeing you around town. Good morning." Vincent tipped his fedora and walked away.

Anna watched, slightly confused. With a small grin, she slowly shut the door.

Vincent approached Domino who was also confused. "What'd you do that for? You had her on the dreambag!"

"No, I was losing her," Vincent said confidently. "She likes me but she's stubborn."

Vincent and Domino gathered their camp from the front lawn as four eyes peaked now and again from the windows. Thinking about it, Domino thought aloud, "Hm. A campaign." They began walking away. "At least you conquered your nerves."

But just as Vincent felt the joy of a small victory, a neighbor's door whipped open and a can of bright blue paint flew out onto the sidewalk. Vincent jumped a mile in the air, frightened. As he took a deep breath with his hand on his heart, he asked exhaustedly, "Where am I?"

CHAPTER SEVEN:
TO A 'T'

Six hours and seventeen minutes later, Anna went into the bathroom to take a shower and get ready for yet another night on the town with Anthony Ceo. She was in the bathroom for 89 minutes. When she emerged from the bathroom door, she saw a human face in her window and jumped two and four-fifths inches off the ground in fright.

Upon closer inspection, she saw that it was an advertisement with Vincent's smiling face on it that read, "The Peddler of Dreams has finally come to Artcity." She giggled as she took the ad down but was amazed to find her front yard was littered with the same advertisement. There were 53 yard signs with Vincent's smiling face in her yard, and one sign per yard throughout the whole neighborhood. As she was looking out, she saw Anthony's shining black convertible pull into her driveway. She closed her curtains and finished getting ready.

Eleven minutes later, she was in Anthony's convertible. With the top down at 53 miles per hour, her hair looked more like antlers than the soft, well-brushed hair of a princess. She asked if Anthony could put the convertible top up so she wouldn't have to show up at the art gallery looking like a Shiras Moose.

Anthony said, "But it's 74 degrees out. It feels amazing. You'll look fine."

Anna sighed.

As they turned the first corner at the end of the street, Anna saw Vincent and Domino in a front lawn pounding a stake into the ground with the advertisement. Vincent noticed the convertible as it approached and turned with a smile on his face and a hand on his hip. Anna giggled to herself and smiled in Vincent's direction. Anthony noticed none of this as he whizzed by.

Anna didn't observe, however, that the moment Anthony's car was beyond her vision of the peddler, Vincent and Domino packed up their remaining yard signs, threw them in a nearby van, and began racing after the convertible. Domino was well trained in finding soul mates, so he kept a safe distance. Anthony never noticed being followed.

Anthony's shining black convertible pulled right up to a red carpet that led from the street to the front doors of the Artcity Subnational Art Gallery. A block away, Domino parked the van and waited for Anthony and Anna to get their pictures taken 94 times before journeying inside.

Vincent and Domino raced to a side entrance where two clowns were holding a service entrance door open for them.

In the front lobby, countless reporters and politicians shook hands with Anthony and bowed to Anna. There were large signs sprinkled all over the lobby that read "Re-elect Congressman Johnson."

Meanwhile, Vincent and Domino had made it through the side door and right out front. Anna was both shocked and impressed to see Vincent. Anthony didn't know him yet, so Anna simply smiled with a roll of her eyes as she walked by him.

Anthony walked directly to Congressman Johnson to pay his respects.

"Good of you to come," Johnson said with an extended hand.

Anthony shook the hand. "I wouldn't miss it, Congressman Johnson. Looks like a good turnout."

"Well it better be. I'm only having three fundraisers this week."

Anna chimed in. "Thanks for inviting us, Scottie. I haven't had time to make it to the Gallery in months."

After twitching at the sound of his name, Johnson faked a smile. "You're very welcome, Anna. I'm so glad you could make it."

Anthony led Anna away to begin viewing some of the paintings, as Johnson continued shaking hands and schmoozing.

Anthony stopped in front of a massive canvas entitled "Fear." "Wow, look at this one, Anna. The brush strokes are so emotional."

Anna turned to face the massive canvas and couldn't stop her face from looking like she had just seen a ghost defecating on her front porch: that rare blend of confusion and disgust, I mean. It looked like the artist had simply taken a house brush full of brown paint and zigzagged downwards. It looked like a kindergartner could have done it. "No," she thought to herself. "Kindergartners have more creative minds than this piece of junk." She noticed the price tag next to the painting. "$13,000."

Vincent was watching from a distance and realized the whole sequence of events. He smiled at finally realizing his soul mate was not one of those crazy, pretentious artist types. Anthony noticed none of this, because he was too swept up in the emotion of the brush strokes. Whether the painting would have had a different effect on him if it was titled "Joy" or "Love," I have no idea.

Anthony wouldn't shut up about the painting for the next hour. He had to have it for his private collection. Anna's tortured thought of actually having to marry this man was suddenly made all the worse by the thought of staring at this ghost poo in her living room. As Anthony made arrangements for the purchase of "Fear," Anna seized the moment to slip away.

She was smiling at a Bouguereau when Vincent nonchalantly whispered over her shoulder, "I thought I'd see you around town."

"Following me is an easy way, peddler."

Vincent laughed. "Following you? Congressman Johnson is a good friend!"

"I think I know all your friends here." Anna pointed at Domino who was a few paintings over with his nose 8 millimeters away from a Cezanne.

As Vincent smiled, he noticed Anthony holding his new painting proudly and showing it off to several admirers, including Congressman Johnson. He said to Anna, "You really like this guy? Look at him."

Anna lowered her head. "He's actually my fiancée."

Vincent felt a small sting in the left side of his chest cavity, but he kept his cool. "No, Anna. You can't marry him."

"And why not?"

"Because you've only just met me. How do you know I'm not the one?"

Anna smiled. "And how do you know that I'm the one?"

Vincent laughed. "I don't know anything... except that I can't seem to stay away from you for very long."

On the other side of the gallery, Congressman Johnson nudged Anthony. "Who's that, talking to Anna?"

Anthony looked over and saw Vincent's lips still inches from Anna's ear. "I have no idea, but I'm about to find out."

But as Anthony took his first step in Vincent's direction, a screeching voice came from a far corner of the Gallery. "And what is this?! How dare they?!" Jaded Summers of the ACCLU stood pointing in outrage at a painting. Anthony and the whole gallery crowded around to see what the fuss was about.

A nervous artist next to her replied, "Uh, what is it, miss?"

Ms. Summers went on, "What on earth is that symbol doing here? That's a cross! A cross in the Subnational Art Gallery! How dare you, sir!"

The nervous artist was confused. "Um, miss? That's a- It's a T. My name is Thomas."

Ms. Summers cut him off. "Well I'd change my name to Homas if I were you, sir. You'll go a lot further in this world. Now take that ghastly painting down."

"Take it down?"

"Of course!" Ms. Summers bellowed. "I will not allow a cross in my public art gallery. Have you ever heard of secularism, sir?"

"But it's just a T. It's the letter T. My name is Thomas."

"Stop arguing with me, Homas. I'm a lawyer. Just take it down."

The nervous artist removed the painting. Jaded Summers was satisfied and moved on.

Domino had journeyed close to the artist to offer some support. "Don't worry, Hummus. We'll hang it back up when she leaves."

"O-Okay."

Anthony looked back over to Anna, but Vincent was gone.

Chapter Eight:
The Theatuh

On a very blue day, a policeman taught a clown various proper security guard postures and etiquettes in front of the world-renowned Theatuh d'Artcity. The policeman was the legendary chief of police, Frank Petrarch, father of true humanism and poet of his beloved Laura, whom I mentioned earlier may or may not have died from an overdose of peanut butter, thanks of course to the lazy health standards of modern corporate factories- a global epidemic.

Chief Petrarch was a cool character. He wore a clean pressed cop suit, properly accessorized, and had a clean short beard, with piercing blue eyes hiding behind black sunglasses. He was the kind of guy that could scream at a baseball umpire and roll his eyes back in joy at a passionate opera in the same day, go back and forth between heavy ales and dry wines, and let a curse word slip but feel guilty for it. He wasn't an average man at all, but had his own distinct style about everything he did, not because he was proud or arrogant, but because he was opinionated and stubborn (a big difference, especially among poets).

The clown he was teaching messed up most of the poses he tried to teach her. As every clown does, she struggled a bit with exaggeration, so when Chief Petrarch showed her a thin, sharp salute, she showed a gaping, waving salute back at him. It was just as Chief Petrarch was practicing a third salute for the clown that Anthony Ceo approached the theatre doors. Anthony was in his trademark tightly tailored three-piece suit, but with the sport jacket draped over his arm.

Without bothering for an introduction, Anthony said shortly, "Is Anna here yet?"

The voice startled Chief Petrarch a bit, but being cool, he wasn't embarrassed at jumping. "Oh- yea, she is, Mr. Ceo."

"Ah, I told you, Chief Petrarch, call me Anthony."

"Oh yea, sorry... Ceo. Anna got here about a half an hour ago."

"Good, good," Anthony responded. "I see you're trying to train a clown. Is she supposed to protect this place or something?"

"She's actually worked here for quite a while," Chief Petrarch informed. Turning to the clown, the Chief continued, "What's it been... about five months or so?-"

"Gelsomina, Anthony, at your service," the clown reached for his hand and shook it with the same amount of exaggeration as the salutes.

"Yes, okay. Call me sir," Anthony said, uncomfortable from the contact.

"Yes, sir Anthony. Sure, sir Anthony," the clown said respectfully. Gelsomina leaned in and whispered to Chief

Petrarch, "I didn't know he was a knight, too. How exciting!"

Chief Petrarch lightly rolled his eyes at the clown's naiveté, as Sir Anthony looked down the street to notice Federico giving a speech to a gathered crowd. Federico, conscious when his nemesis entered his proximity, smiled back at Anthony's disturbed glance.

Anthony stormed in the theatre doors.

Alone again, Chief Petrarch made Gelsomina focus on the security guard poses.

Just beyond Federico's crowd, Domino and Vincent came strolling down the street. Vincent was in the middle of a question. "But how powerful could he be? You clowns don't seem to be embraced so cordially around here."

Domino explained, "Yea, but Federico's from a powerful lineage. His family used to rule Artcity, back before Anthony took over the Corporation."

Domino hushed Vincent's inquisitive response as they joined the crowd and listened to Federico's speech.

Federico was saying, "Businessmen have seized our city. They've rebelled from everything this great city used to stand for. They live and breathe now only for money, only for the self-gratification of a large, dust-gathering bank account.

"Don't you see then, brothers and sisters? They *have* to hold us back! They *have* to refuse us! Because if we succeed, if we can rise, we threaten everything they stand for. The people don't care about money. They can't put Cloud bills (pulling a Cloud bill that is raining from his pocket, and throwing it on the ground) in a frame and admire them- they don't think about painting pennies red- They don't care about that stuff! The people won't pay businessmen their hard-earned money for painted money.

"And the businessmen have only money. They had to take over the arts. They took over the artists who control what the people really want. They took what has always been the interest of the people: the obsession, the celebration and the lament- of life. They have stolen the art from Artcity!"

Federico paused for a moment, as he looked down and wiped the light sweat that had gathered on his cheeks-obviously the sweat came off but not the paint. He looked back at his crowd and continued, "We have to fight back, clowns. We have to show them- and the people- what we live for. Otherwise, we might as well believe in their easy ideals and convenient laws and give up the discipline and the hard work of chasing perfection that we call life."

As Federico continued, Domino whispered something in Vincent's ear, pointing at the theatre as Chief Petrarch walked away from Gelsomina and down the street. Vincent was obviously pleased and a little excited by the news. They left the crowd, and approached the sidewalk where Gelsomina was still practicing her security guard poses.

Gelsomina shouted out, "Hi, Domino!"

Domino responded lifelessly, "Hey, Gelsomina."

Gelsomina continued excitedly, "And who's your new friend?"

"This is Vincent Fides," Domino presented. "Mr. Fides, Gelsomina."

Vincent shook Gelsomina's hand energetically, surprising even her. "The peddler of dreams."

Gelsomina's face vibrated with the shaking. "Ooo. Okay."

Domino asked slyly, "Is Anna in there?"

"Oh yes, Domino," Gelsomina said proudly. "But you know I can't let you in. I'm the security guard! And I take my responsibilities very, very seriously, you know."

"Oh I know that... sweetheart," Domino said slyly.

"Ooo, sweetheart?" Gelsomina sighed.

Vincent nodded at Domino. Domino sighed back with discomfort.

Domino continued, "Gelsomina... darling. I was hoping we could talk privately for a minute."

"Ooo, darling! Sure, Domino, anything!" Gelsomina was swooning.

Domino turned to Vincent dramatically, "Would you please excuse us, Mr. Fides?" He then put his arm around Gelsomina and tried to walk her away from the door.

But Gelsomina didn't budge. She looked back at the door she was supposed to be guarding. "No, wait, Domino," she realized. "Excuse him."

Vincent acted offended, "No, excuse me!"

"No, excuse us!" Gelsomina threw her arm around Domino and led him away from Vincent, and subsequently, away from the door she was supposed to be guarding.

Vincent watched with a smile as Domino began talking seriously to Gelsomina. He began liking the clowns even more. He looked at the door, thought of Anna, and rushed in.

Inside, Vincent crept through the shadows of the house seats, as Anthony's rehearsal was mid-scene.

Anna wore a Shakespearean corset and dress, her hands flailing tragically yet beautifully, as Mephistopheles, dressed as Voltaire, swayed through her library door.

Anna Fausta sang desperately as she collapsed to the floor, "What then is truth?"

Mephistopheles sang triumphantly and slyly, "I should then have said to Pilate:—Historical truths are merely probabilities. If you had fought at the battle of Philippi, that is for you a truth which you know by intuition, by perception. But for us who dwell near the Syrian desert, it is merely a very probable thing, which we know by hearsay. How much hearsay is necessary to form a conviction equal to that of a man who, having seen the thing, can flatter himself that he has a sort of certainty?"

Anna Fausta answered, "But is not even experience to be valuable in forming our personhood of choices? And what of trust?"

Mephistopheles sang on, "He who has heard the thing told by twelve thousand eyewitnesses, has only twelve thousand probabilities, equal to one strong probability, which is not equal to certainty. If you have the thing from only one of these witnesses, you know nothing; you should be sceptical. If the witness is dead, you should be still more sceptical, for you cannot enlighten yourself. If from several witnesses who are dead, you are in the same plight. If from those to whom the witnesses have spoken, your scepticism should increase still more."

Anna Fausta curled in a ball on the floor, "Then it is chaos you dare to offer me as my humanity? And in trade for my soul I should accept your humanism of chaos?"

Mephistopheles concluded, "From generation to generation scepticism increases, and probability diminishes; and soon probability is reduced to zero."[4]

Suddenly Screwtape, dressed as Nietzsche, flew in from the wings, his voice booming at his rival Mephistopheles, "If we make it clear to any one that, strictly, he can never speak of truth, but only of probability and of its degrees, we generally discover, from the undisguised joy of our pupil, how greatly men prefer the uncertainty of their intellectual horizon, and how in their heart of hearts they hate truth because of its definiteness. — Is this due to a secret fear felt by all that the light of truth may at some time be turned too brightly upon themselves? To their wish to be of some consequence, and accordingly their concealment from the world of what they are? Or is it to be traced to their horror of the all-too brilliant light, to which their crepuscular, easily dazzled, bat-like souls are not accustomed, so that hate it they must?"[5]

Anna Fausta cried from her ball, "No, not both of you! I cannot decide this now!"

Mephistopheles would not be outdone. He shoved Screwtape down to the ground and with his long fingers caressed Anna's hair, "Delightenment thought, my dear!"

"Enlightenment you mean!" Anna Fausta boomed back, rising to her feet as a soldier who's discovered a spy.

"That's what I said!" Mephistopheles sang on the defensive.

Screwtape seized the opportunity, "Pilate, with his question, 'What is Truth?' is now gleefully brought on the scene as an advocate of Christ, in order to cast suspicion on all that is known or knowable as being mere appearance, and to erect the Cross on the appalling background of the Impossibility of Knowledge."[6]

Anna Fausta sang back, "Then grant me equality as the magicians and citizens do!"

But Screwtape cowered, "What is this mania for counting noses?"[7]

Mephistopheles rose again, "Then choose me, my dear!"

"No, choose me, my dear!" came Screwtape's challenge.

Vincent watched intently as Anna Fausta looked back and forth between the two devils. Anthony Ceo rose from his seat, a thin bamboo cane swaying to the music as he awaited a sort of culmination to his anxiety.

Both devils looked at Anna with expectation. Anna felt the devils' peering eyes baking her skin with heat. She didn't know what to say, though. The script didn't matter anymore. Anthony watched on, captivated by her assumed acting.

But finally, Anna broke character with an exhausted sigh. "I can't do it, Anthony. Why should I choose this one over that one? They're both wrong."

"Blasphemy!" Anthony shouted, offended by his actress' assumption. "How dare you say Voltaire is wrong! Nietzsche maybe, but Voltaire?! Act the scene, Anna!"

"But it doesn't make any sense," Anna contended. "I mean, they're both skeptics. And, no offense, but if I have to choose between isolated rationalism and superman, I would choose superman."

Anthony loved the challenge. "But you miss the point of the whole scene, Anna! Voltaire is not offering you a life lived free from conscience, only a life liberated from preconceived structures. It is freedom- true freedom at last."

Anna shook her head. "You call chaos freedom? Freedom is not simply a lack of boundaries, but the right use of our free will."

But Anthony boomed back. "Free will bounded by morality or ethics or prejudices or preconceptions? Free will demands chaos- If there is a lack of choice, then there is a lack of freedom!"

Anna genuinely didn't understand how Anthony could think that freedom could be gained from a lack of restrictions. "But whatever you choose will indeed bound you and enslave you. You call it freedom to live without restraint, but you only invite more masters to chain you up. If no rules govern sex, and you live excessively, exercising your so-called 'freedom,' then that's not freedom at all. Sex will enslave you where the rules did not."

It was when Anthony began speaking about the difference between Neoclassicists and Romantics that Anna noticed Vincent hiding in the back of the house. She giggled a bit, which annoyed Anthony mid-argument, but she didn't give the intruder over to her authority.

Back out front, Domino led Gelsomina around the other side of the building to the front again. "And that's why it's so important for our clowns to hold important positions. I guess what I'm trying to say is, well, I'm proud of you, Gelsomina."

Gelsomina was very touched. "Oh, thank you, Domino. You know your opinion has always meant the world to me. I do consider you (she leaned in to wink) one of my closest friends."

Domino changed the subject sharply, "Uh, where's Vincent?!"

Gelsomina was startled. "Well, he- We went- Oh, who cares, Domino? As long as you and I are-"

"I'm worried about him, Gelsomina. What if he- Oh, no!"

Gelsomina looked at the door. "You don't think he went in the theatre, do you?"

"He must have," came Domino's reply. "We'll have to find him quietly."

The two went in after Vincent.

Back inside, Anthony Ceo was quoting Voltaire, one of his favorite ways of showing off. Anthony went on to dismiss Anna's ideas as naive and innocent, based purely on magic and superstition and two millennia of so-called indoctrination, one of his favorite words though he did not know the difference between the so-called indoctrination of their stories and the indoctrination of his own propaganda.

Anna knew she was never supposed to do what she was about to do, that what she was about to do was quite possibly the greatest (in size and value) possible insult she could ever offer a Delightenment stinker- excuse me, Enlightenment thinker. But nevertheless, rebel that she was, she did it. She quoted Aquinas!

"Behold our refutation of the error. It is not based on documents of faith, but on the reasons and statements of the philosophers themselves. If then anyone there be who, boastfully taking pride in his supposed wisdom, wishes to challenge what we have written, let him not do it in some corner nor before children who are powerless to decide on such difficult matters. Let him reply openly if he dare. He shall find me there confronting him, and not only my negligible self, but many another whose study is truth. We shall do battle with his errors or bring a cure to his ignorance."[8]

Anthony's skin began sweating with discomfort throughout the quotation. When she finished and stood staring at him, he rolled his eyes and said, "Ugh, a Dominican?"

In a sound booth on the second floor, overlooking the stage and the argument below, Domino rooted through boxes of wiring, while Gelsomina looked under a couch and a coffee table. Gelsomina was confused, though. "But I don't think he's in here, Domino. In fact, I'm quite sure of it."

"Ssh. We have to play a joke on someone," Domino said as he found the proper wire he had been looking for.

"Ooo- a joke?" Gelsomina whispered excitedly.

"Sssh! You don't wanna get in trouble, do you?" Domino chastised.

Below, Anthony Ceo had retreated from faith and reason, but substituted a tirade against Thomism in general, and the clowns to be more specific.

Suddenly, Federico's booming voice came sweeping through the theatre from every speaker in the house. Federico said, "Church and State may of course be separate, as both the Church and the State will plainly tell you, but this separation can only be institutional. For the separation of Church and State has never meant the separation of faith and State. To pretend that a man or woman of faith can approach policies without their convictions and answers to life's largest questions is not only naive but hopeless. And further, and more importantly, if a State is unable or unwilling to approach such questions that religion has always attempted to answer, they are left futile and ineffective in any true government. Put simply, if a State cannot even define human life, how can they govern human life? This is the purpose of the faithful in a nation, to provide true dialogue. If the faithful are denied access to that national dialogue, then the State is inevitably atheistic, as much by its own isolation from religion as from its own proclamation of and unification around nihilism."

During the speech, Anthony raced out of the theatre to confront the clown for interrupting his rehearsal. Vincent seized the moment of distraction and freedom to travel towards the stage and his beloved Anna Fausta. They both heard Federico's speech interrupted by the approaching Anthony.

"Federico! Why are you interrupting my rehearsal, you dog?"

"What's that you're complaining about now? I didn't realize I was interrupting anything, Ceo. I'm obeying the ordinance- This is at least 500 feet," Federico defended himself.

"How did you get on my intercom if you didn't go in the theatuh first?" Anthony replied.

As Vincent approached the stage, he called up to the sound booth, "Domino! Turn it off, man."

The intercom fell silent, but Gelsomina suddenly realized the entire sequence of events. She raced out of the booth to catch Vincent before Anthony returned.

Vincent was preoccupied, though. "Hey, you're a pretty good dancer. Maybe you could teach me a step or two?"

Anna calmly warned, "What are you doing here? Anthony'll kill you when he gets back."

Vincent ignored the warning. "What's the name of this junk? It's pretty depressing."

Anna took a deep breath before saying, "Tormented Atoms in a Bed of Mud: A Philosophical Musical."

Vincent thought it over. "Horrible title... It's a musical, huh?"

Anna was slightly offended. "Is there something wrong with musicals?"

"No, no... not a-tall," Vincent mocked.

Anna was slightly more offended, "They happen to be the greatest contribution to the theatre of the 20th century-"

But Vincent said quickly, "What's that tell ya?"

"That they capture and represent the interest of an era!" Anna responded.

"Ah, the era. Right," Vincent mocked playfully.

"They do!" Anna was playfully defensive.

Vincent interrupted her again, "I'm not gonna argue about the modern state of the theatre with you. I get it, I get it: Stanislavsky, Artaud, *Anything Goes*. Right."

Anna wasn't sure if it was more the paradox of Stanislavsky and Artaud mentioned together, or Artaud and *Anything Goes* mentioned together, that made her laugh, but she did to Vincent's delight. Anna continued, "Well it *is* a horrible title. An Anthony Ceo original no less."

Vincent couldn't stop his eyes from rolling. "Everybody thinks they can write these days."

Anna noticed the security clown rush through the door from the stairwell. "He will kill you when he comes back, you know."

"Oh don't worry about that dork- he isn't worth your time."

"And you are?" Anna asked.

"I will be," Vincent proclaimed confidently.

"Oh," Anna chuckled. "And when exactly will that be?"

Vincent began shifting through his dreambag. "When I can figure out what I've got in this bag that could make you mine."

"You want to own me?" Anna asked, which was of course all a modern woman would have heard in such a remark.

Vincent thought it over, knowing well the implications of what he said. He decided. "Yes, I do."

Gelsomina rushed onto the stage. Out of breath and panting, she said, "Vincent Fides, the peddler of dreams, you gotta get outta here!"

But Vincent wasn't done yet. "Not now, Gelsomina. Gimme a minute."

Anna continued, "I'm not for sale, peddler."

Vincent shot back, "I'm not offering money in exchange here, only the very same in return."

"Oh, I could own you?" Anna surmised.

"You already do, sweetheart. That's why I'm here," Vincent said confidently.

Gelsomina looked back and forth with every reply until she shook her head. "Hey! Is the security guard standing here?!" Gelsomina looked around, first left, then right, everybody on stage following her glances. Finally, she noticed her own badge and pretended to be startled. "Oh! I'm the security guard!" Gelsomina winked proudly at Domino who had ventured near the stage.

Vincent responded, "Yes, I apologize, Gelsomina. I got lost outside, and I... wandered inside." He didn't realize how foolish it sounded till it was sounded, so he tried to cover it up. "Anna's a good friend of mine."

Anthony Ceo was walking down the center aisle. "I thought I knew all of your friends, Anna. Can I help you, young man? We're trying to rehearse."

"Young man?" Vincent said sarcastically. "And how old are you?" He turned to Anna coolly, "Who is this guy?"

"Who am I?" Anthony was visibly offended. "I'm Anthony Ceo-"

Gelsomina leaned in and whispered to Vincent, "Sir Anthony. He's a knight."

Anthony continued, "I'm the man who owns this theatuh, and this town. Who the hell are you?"

Vincent chuckled. "Say 'theatre' again."

Anthony boomed, "What?!"

Vincent jumped down from the stage to approach Anthony. Tipping his hat, he said, "Oh, nothing. I'm Vincent Fides, the peddler of dreams."

Anthony had had enough of the newcomer. He turned to Gelsomina, "And where were you?!"

Gelsomina pointed in a couple different directions, "Well, I, uh- I was…"

Anthony continued, "He's probably stealing the set ideas, the lighting, everything!- Get him out of here!"

Vincent turned back towards Anna and winked before beginning a slow pace down the center aisle. "Oh, no. I couldn't care less about that stuff… I'm actually stealing your star." Vincent kept walking and never looked back.

Anthony was still visibly frustrated as Gelsomina ran to catch up with Vincent. Anthony yelled, "You're fired… Jell-… Je-… Whoever you are!"

Vincent and Gelsomina exited the theatre as Domino snuck out to join them at the door.

Anthony wanted to sit down, but was still too rattled to sit still. He paced back and forth, and then stood with folded arms, looking at where he was supposed to sit down. Finally, when he thought the others had gone and therefore could not hear him, he said to Anna, "What were you two talking about?"

Anna was delighted to see Anthony in such a frazzled state. "Nothing… sir. Let's get back to work."

Anthony wouldn't let it go, though. "What do you mean nothing? What'd he say?"

After a short pause, Anna smiled. "That he wants to own me."

Anthony looked at the ground, at the door, at the chair, at the wings, at the ground. "Own you? Yea." He let out a forced chuckle.

After another moment, he sat down. The players on the stage got in their places to restart the scene. Anthony said under his breath, "Theatuh. Theatre... er. er."

CHAPTER NINE:
A SHINE

"But you have to understand, Mr. Fides," Domino said. "It's not just magic and old stories. It's the sacramental life and new stories, always new. It's *their* way that's the old way, the ugliness of hedonism and nihilism and narcissism and relativism. They give you handsome statues, sure, but they're made of chalk and wither away at the slightest touch, even at the feathery touch of the wind. They are mere fashions, as lasting as the single generations that support them. The statues in our formation are made of marble, strong and ageless, but gentle enough to be formed by the Good Sculptor."

As Domino and Vincent Fides walked along a sidewalk, Vincent thought about all Domino had been saying and finally shook his head. He said, "No, Domino. Magic, sacraments, it's all the same to me. Why should I let your way 'form' (he said that word with great suspicion) me any more than I should let them? I'm me. I may be dumb sometimes- I mean, I know I am far from perfect, but I follow my heart. I form myself."

Domino grinned dismissively. "Then tell me this, hotshot. How much have you sold here in Artcity?" There was silence, so Domino continued, "Have you sold anything but college degrees? You were only selling those at $50K- Of course you'll sell those easily. But anything else? One single, solitary little thing? A magic-filled cane or a dancing flower?"

Vincent didn't like that question. "Shut up," he said, avoiding it.

Domino continued, "I'm not trying to be hurtful, Mr. Fides- I want to prove a point. It's not entirely your fault that your efforts are futile here. You've only come up with the idea that you're a good peddler by acting like something you're not. You sell Artcity merchandise to the outside world. Big deal. The Artcity arts sell themselves. But now you've come here, and you suddenly realize that what you've been, or at least what you think you've been, doesn't work, doesn't fit in. So you've got to find a way to be a better person, a better peddler. Now I'm not arguing that the Good Sculptor wants to form you into a Moses or a David, or a Venus for that matter, but Anthony's not stupid enough to pitch you those identities either. The devil's greatest trick was not to convince the world that he doesn't exist- even the world isn't so foolish. The devil's greatest trick is to convince you that you've got plenty of time to change later. As a great African clown said, 'Change me, O Lord... but not yet.'[9]

"No, you are forming yourself indeed, Mr. Fides, every moment of every day, with every glance, gesture, and decision you make. What the Universals can do is show you how to become the best possible version of you. The other side only wants you to sink to their level, to think like they think, so then they can cling to the most powerful excuse they've ever employed: 'Everybody else does it, thinks it, wants it, lives for it, dies for it.' The moment you do more, think more, want more, live for more, and die for more- that's the moment you become a challenge to them- that's the moment that they have to feel guilt. And they'll do anything to avoid guilt. In a sad sort of way, it comes down to that, Mr. Fides. I know you'll be you, scars and flaws and all, but will you measure yourself to them or to the best possible version of you? Don't you see? It is our side that shows humanism- their side shows only obstacles and stumbling blocks to your progress as an individual. They don't know what individualism means, only hedonism. They don't know what freedom means, only license. They don't know what a man can be, only what a man can get."

The two were quiet for about seventeen paces.

Finally, Domino said, "That's the jail up there."

Atop the jail was a beautiful woman named Mary who dangled her legs over the side of the roof. Mary was talking to Chief Petrarch who stood below her at the jail's entrance. Mary said, "I resent that. I work hard up here, Chief Petrarch, and I only give people who deserve to get out the key!"

Chief Petrarch boomed back, "I decide who deserves in or out!"

Just then a man in a bright red, hooded robe with a hooked nose walked up. Looking up, he threw a rose atop the jail and said,

"Fairest thou where all are fair!

Plead with Christ our sins to spare!"[10]

Mary smiled largely, "Hey Dante honey!" She tossed down a key, and then continued her defense against the police. "I run a perfectly legal business, Chief. I pay my rent. I-"

"To who?!" Chief Petrarch screamed.

The customer slipped past the police chief on the sidewalk. "Excuse me, Petrarch."

Knowing the man well, the Chief replied, "Excuse me, Dante."

Mary answered, "To the Mayor... obviously! This is public property, ya know."

Chief Petrarch continued, "Mary, you give keys to the jail to people who have just been arrested. Last week, Francis Thompson escaped- I don't quite understand how you think this is a perfectly legal business."

A strangely dressed Elizabethan walked up with tights and a handlebar. He threw a rose on the roof, and shouted,

"Fairest thou where all are fair!

Plead with Christ our sins to spare!"

Mary tossed down a key as she continued, "It's not like you have a copyright on your locks, Chief. They're public domain."

Frustrated and stumped by this response, the Chief called into the jail. "Peire! Peire!"

After a moment, a jester-looking troubadour stepped out of the jail with a badge that read, Deputy Peire d'Alvernhe. "Yea, Chief?"

Chief Petrarch screamed angrily, "Call down to the Mayor's office. I need a copyright on these locks, and all of the keys, too."

Mary screamed down, "No! You can't! You can't- I'll do it first!-"

Peire looked up at Mary, then back at Chief Petrarch. "You want a copyright... on our keys?"

Petrarch boomed back before the words were even out of the deputy's mouth, "Yes! Now!"

Peire was dumbfounded. "O-Okay." He slowly went back into the jail.

Mary was wailing, "I'll be out of business, on the street. Are you happy? Taking a girl's greatest honor in service!"

The Elizabethan gentleman, who had stopped to watch the dispute with interest, walked away with key in hand. Chief Petrarch, standing there about to explode, attacked the customer, fighting over the key, and finally ripped it away from him and kicked him on the behind.

The Elizabethan gentleman rushed off. Chief Petrarch reentered the jail, slamming the door behind him.

Vincent and Domino had continued walking, a little too frightened to stop for too long. They caught much of the event as any witness of a domestic dispute listens closely while trying very hard to act as if they can't hear what's going on at all. Domino explained to Vincent Mary's purpose in life and how anyone who asked her for a key would certainly get one but how most people didn't even know that she had keys, and that she was generous enough to give them freely, much to the Chief's dismay.

They kept walking though, because Domino wasn't leading Vincent Fides to the jail. He was leading him back to Rustici Palace, for today, Vincent had an appointment.

As Domino led Vincent past the booth of Jaded Summers, ACCLU, Ms. Summers did a little magic trick, making a card disappear from her wide-open hands. "I can do some things, too, Mr. Fides," she said with a grin as they passed.

Neither Domino nor Vincent paid her any mind, though. Domino stopped at the entrance, as Vincent Fides continued on into the open-air Palace. He walked right up to the shoe-shine chair which the Sage of Rustici Palace gestured towards with a welcoming towel. As Vincent sat down, the Sage wasted no time with introductions. "Heya, Vincent!" the Sage exclaimed.

Vincent was obviously uneasy. "I don't know what to call you. Mr. Sage? His Royalness? What?"

"Royalness? Plain ol' 'Sage' sounds like a name," the Sage said while he bent down to begin studying Vincent's shoes with extreme precision.

"I guess I shouldn't be surprised that you know my name?" Vincent asked.

"It was on the appointment book, Mista Fides. I heard you were a bright one."

Vincent felt dumb, as he should have of course, but the Sage knew what he was after. The Sage continued, "Anyways, how could I escape yer name? Everyone's talkin' 'boutcha." Vincent still didn't know how to respond. The Sage continued, "'Specially ma friend, Jaded Summers, ova there."

"What's her deal? She gives me the creeps," Vincent said uncomfortably.

The Sage chuckled. "She's a pansy at heart, I assure ya. Airbody may have an opinion, but that don't make it tha truth. Truth's tha only opinion that really matters, right? I think sometimes, when ya pack yer brain so tight with a bunch a junk that don't matter much, stuff starts poppin' out tha other side, know what I mean?"

After a pause in which Vincent really did think about it, he said dully, "No."

The Sage wasn't listening to Vincent's response, though. "Other people been talkin', too, much more important people than that troubled soul ova there."

Vincent was baited. "What's the Mayor saying?"

The Sage smiled. As he whipped out a fresh rag and began scuffing the sides of Vincent's shoes, he asked, "Ya really care what the Mayor thinks?"

Vincent replied honestly, "Yea. He's still her father."

The Sage shot back, "The only man more confident than a politician is a lunatic. Don't look for his approval."

Vincent didn't like that answer. "I want his approval."

"'N you could only get it by doin' what he's prayin' you can't do."

"What's that?" Vincent asked.

"Peddle some dreams here in Artcity, of course," the Sage said proudly.

Vincent laughed. "Give me a break- I'm not an idiot. You guys already have everything here. I can't compete. I'm sold out of college degrees- I knew I should've sold them for more."

The Sage suddenly sounded more serious. "Maybe it's paradise to you, Mista Fides, but everybody else may still need ya. Why're ya still here if you've got nothin' ta sell?"

Vincent sighed. "I've tried and tried, Sage, but nothing I do seems to work. Nobody needs me here- I just don't think this is where I belong."

"Then where ezactly do ya belong?"

Quietly, Vincent said, "I don't know."

The Sage smiled real big. "You're no different than most the people out there in this world, brother. Nobody knows where they fit in. But I tell, Mista Fides, and ya gotta believe me: no matter how distraught ya get, how frustrated ya get at every turn- you know, when every single little thing ya try gets thrown right back in yer face- then, and especially then, ya gotta keep believin' in yerself.

If it starts gettin' hard, that's when you know that yer close."

Vincent shook his head is disagreement. "But how, Sage? I mean it's easy to say that- it's even easy to believe it. But when you're faced with defeat at every turn, and it feels like nothing you do can ever change it, how can you believe in yourself? I mean, if there's absolutely nothing, not a single outward sign from absolutely anyone outside your own mind telling you that you matter, that you're on the right path, that though things are hard for now, there's a brighter day ahead- when you're in the middle of a desert, how can you hope?"

"Ah, Mista Fides, ya hit it squarely. It's about hope then, yea? Does hope come from the inside or the outside?"

Vincent didn't understand. "You mean, is hope found inside the person or is it given by other people?"

The Sage smiled, "That sounds about right."

Vincent thought it over while the Sage broke out fresh rags to start dusting off his shine. Finally, Vincent said, "I suppose it comes from the inside. Otherwise, it wouldn't really be hope. If it came from the outside, the very thing that would provide the hope would be called evidence, and hope would actually be a certainty, which hope is not."

The Sage smiled even bigger as he stood up. "'Atta boy, Mista Fides. It's gotta come from the inside, 'n it's gotta come when there ain't enough evidence to be certain. If there was enough evidence, what would ya need hope for?"

Vincent shook his head again, "But I've tried everything, Sage. Artcing was fine before I came and it'll be the same long after I leave."

"Then I repeat, why ya still here? Tryin' to catch somethin' for yerself maybe?" The Sage stretched a little from being on his knees.

Vincent smiled, "Well, sure, but... I hope she gets something out of it, too. I just don't know what I have to give."

"'N Domino?" the Sage asked with a smile.

Vincent chuckled. "Yea, and Domino."

"'N the clowns?" the Sage asked with an even bigger smile.

Vincent was confused, though. "The clowns? How could I-?"

But the Sage interrupted him. "Jus' checkin'." Then as if reading his fortune, "Vincent Fides, the peddler of dreams... I suggest ya stick to yer forte. Whatever ya got-in or out of that dreambag of yers- you gotta start peddlin'. 'Sides, if it don't terrify you, it's probly not worth doin'. You gotta learn that everybody here's no different than anywhere else in one respect: we may *have* a bunch a figurines and whatever else you been tryin' ta peddle here, but life ain't about whatcha got, it's about who ya are, know what I mean?"

Domino watched intently, as the Sage bent down again to finish up Vincent's shine without another word. Vincent thought intently about what if anything he could ever offer to these people.

Chapter Ten:
White from Black

In the bright green office high above Artcity, the Mayor sat upright and on the edge of his tall leather chair, screaming into a telephone. "I don't care what it takes, pipsqueak! You get that wanderer's mind off my little girl!"

Anthony Ceo said, "It's not that easy, Mayor. I can't even get to him- the clowns protect him."

"The clowns? Clowns? They've been runnin' circles around you for weeks- that's *your* problem. Get me Fides!" The Mayor stood up, pacing behind his desk like a lion in a cage.

"I'm trying, Mayor," Anthony began. "I just need some time. I've got people following your daughter everywhere. He's sure to pop up sooner or later."

"Following my daughter? She doesn't need to be dragged into-"

But Anthony interrupted him. "I think we're both getting a little desperate here, sir. There's no time to hold back. Maybe now you can see that if you hadn't allowed Federico and the clowns to gain this momentum-"

"Stop it! Don't you dare criticize me, boy. Yea, I've got some things at stake to take, but no more or less than you and your mistakes have taken for money's sake. Forget your stupid play and bring that peddler to me now!"

Anthony was confused. "What, you want to talk to him?"

The Mayor screamed, "Of course I do!" and slammed the phone down. The Mayor just stood there for a moment, not ready to sit down, and not ready for a contemplative gaze out the window. He just stood there, burning the phone with his fiery eyes.

Far below, in the City Circle, Anna walked along a sidewalk window shopping for clothes or shoes or music or anything else that might have caught her eye. She wore a bright orange and red summer dress, the pinstripes bent and overlapping to form a fun floral pattern, but without any hippie overtones.

Vincent Fides, the peddler of dreams, was admiring the floral pattern at a safe distance, watching her intently. He wanted the perfect opportunity to surprise her, his primary device in the campaign. So as she noticed a cool vintage hat in a window, and entered the store, Vincent decided to make his move. He ran up and sat on an adjacent park bench near the store's entrance.

He plopped down and acted like he wasn't paying very close attention to the door opening behind him. When it did, he looked back hurriedly, but his gallant smile fell as he found a young woman in a business suit instead.

Smith couldn't help but chuckle. As Vincent turned back around, Smith walked over and sat down right next to Vincent, to Vincent's surprise.

"You were expecting someone else," Smith said with a smile.

Vincent didn't recognize her from the first time he saw the Sage. "Yea, I'm sorry," Vincent replied.

"She is quite beautiful," Smith added.

"Who?" Vincent asked dumbly.

"Anna, of course."

Vincent smiled. "Ah. We haven't properly met yet. I'm Vincent Fides, the peddler of dreams," he said with an extended hand.

Smith took the hand firmly. "Smith."

"That's it? Smith?"

Smith was confused. "What do you mean?"

"You got a first name?"

"Oh- It is- Well, it is Marie," Smith answered uncomfortably.

"Marie Smith! There we go. Pleasure to meet you. Now, are you Anthony's or the Mayor's?" Vincent asked.

"I hold a unique position in the Corporation."

"Anthony's, great. What do you do exactly?" Vincent continued.

Smith didn't have much time, though. "That's not important, Mr. Fides. For reasons I cannot disclose, I want to inform you of something. I need you to know that you are being watched. Whenever you go near her: know that someone is reporting everything you do."

"Why would you tell me?" Vincent was confused.

"Let us just say that I have a personal investment in your success. I would appreciate it if you never mentioned to anyone what we have spoken about. Good day, Mr.

Fides." And Smith calmly arose and walked away without looking back.

"Wait- Marie!" Vincent called to no avail.

Vincent forgot about why he was sitting there, and began looking around in all directions, like a bull's eye with a whole squadron of sharp-shooters ready to snipe him at any moment. Just as he began to freak out, Anna began to open the door of the shop behind him, but recognized the brown fedora on the park bench. She rushed back into the store to write a little note. A moment later, she returned and exited the store swiftly. Vincent turned, his eyes almost as wide as their first meeting, but they creased quickly when she darted off, dropping a piece of paper on the ground behind her.

He rose quickly. "Anna!" He picked up the paper with a smile, thinking she had accidentally dropped it, a receipt, a grocery list, a prospectus for a new book. He took seven steps chasing her. "Anna, you dropped-" Realizing suddenly that the piece of paper was not lost but placed, he looked around again, remembering the snipers. He hid the piece of paper in a pocket, and very inconspicuously walked away from Anna to find a private place to sit and read his note.

He sat on the Wine Fountain's ledge, where dozens of others who seemed to be on their lunch break leaned over the edge with their plastic cups to draw their vino while they ate burgers or pasta or burritos. Vincent took one last sweeping investigation of his surroundings until he felt safe. And just as he opened his note to read it, a funeral procession walked slowly by him, a carnival of black following a humble box of humbler dust, the same kind of box magicians tell volunteers to step inside, just before an incredible trick.

The note read, 'Peddler, they would never let us be together. Please, I think you should leave me alone. A.'

Something inside Vincent died at that moment. Maybe it was his invincibility, or his naiveté, or his innocence, or his inexperience, something colorless and shapeless, but far more important than anything material. For the first time in his life, he considered a potential life without his wildest dreams come true. For the first time in his life, he realized that life doesn't happen to you- you have to make it happen yourself.

And just as Vincent Fides, the peddler of dreams, began seeing the world in a very different light, and a much brighter light, a new procession went by in the opposite direction. These were happier and brighter people, a desert of white following a little crowned statue of a beautiful woman. They sang happily and danced in the streets. And something inside Vincent was born anew, fresh, never existing before that precise moment, and every ounce of his energy danced in his bones. He realized he was alive. And he realized that he could in fact be all he had ever dreamed of being. He had never known such a peace before, and yet he recognized it- it felt like home. Such a feeling is quite common at the moment that a vocation is realized. Being a 'recognition,' it occurs from the outside, as one is not yet living the life he sees plainly before him, just as a sailor recognizes his life from the shore, a moment before plunging into the water. Vincent saw his place in the world, and realized his life had been in his own hands all along.

Chapter Eleven:
The Blueprints

The cold, damp lair of the clowns' operation hub had the feel of a century-old circus tent. The bright colors had faded decades ago. The walls were lined with old vintage posters of famous clowns on vaudeville circuits that have become in recent years highways and interstates lined with corporate chains that are just as unimpressive in quality as they are impressive in quantity. Yes, the famous clowns were dead and buried. The monuments of Clown Town were confined to the cemeteries, like so many great American towns and villages. But Clown Town had a greatness of her own that could not be touched. Every community has a type of soul, though not in the theological sense, and Clown Town had a very big soul that no corporate chain, interstate, or popular culture could ever kill.

The clowns loved their home, and though it was run down, short of water, energy, public transportation, and public services, the clowns knew they had what once was the nicest community in the metropolitan Artcity area. Nowhere else were ten foot ceilings, original woodwork, and precise craftsmanship in such abundance, even if such foundations had grown old and frail in recent decades. The clowns were proud of their home, and they took good care of her. The cold, damp lair was Federico's home, the very home Federico's famous father had been born and raised in.

In the center of the large room with faded bright colors was an antique desk, taller and more beautiful than the Mayor's, at which sat Federico himself, the gallant hero and voice of his generation, the stubborn brat that no amount of criticism could deflate, the scapegoat that Anthony's power relied on.

Federico was at the piano, the melody filling the house. While Federico played, several clowns hovered over his desk with blueprints, one set of blueprints for a building, another set of blueprints for a revolution. They whispered of possible ways to infiltrate the Corporation's hold on Artcity's resources.

Federico began to sing in the rough and hoarse voice of a masterful pianist who sings only out of necessity.

"Beauty,
whether that of the natural universe
or that expressed in art,
precisely because it opens up
and broadens the horizons of human awareness,
pointing us beyond ourselves,
bringing us face to face with the abyss of Infinity,
can become a path towards the transcendent,

towards the ultimate Mystery,
towards God."[11]

Another clown walked in from the dining room- he announced loudly over Federico's music, "Behold the lamb. Blessed are those called to this supper." And Federico and the clowns all scurried quickly into the next room.

Chapter Twelve: The Rise & Fall of J.J. Banker

Once upon a time in a distant and exotic land, a mother gave birth to the first Banker, and as a result, Pangaea shattered into four distinct continents that exploded away from each other on tectonic plates. This is how the world that we know has come to be, with the birth of the Bankers. They were a curious breed of human from the start, always lookin' for a buck, or a Cloud bill, or whatever the local currency. Money was like food to them- they needed it for human energy purposes. They've yet to understand really the process of circulation, for their whole aim and understanding of life is to get more, and then more, and then more. They consume everything they can, similar to the moving force of lava. And like lava, they leave a dirty residue wherever they go- indeed, they have changed many landscapes throughout the history of human civilization.

And yet I wonder if it is quite proper to call them 'human,' for they do not at all resemble any other form or race within humanity. Perhaps they are simply a different race, but not a race based on mere colorations and pigments in our organic skins (how trifling a measurement of a man's character that has always been anyway). No, this race is like when the sci-fi geeks talk about a race of robots or zombies or aliens, a race defined precisely by their distance from humans. I do not mean to demean or belittle their heritage (they're not a race you want as enemies), but I only mean to point out that they exist only in their office, or purpose, or functionality to the robot they represent. A bank is not a human thing, so neither are the Bankers that sacrifice their humanity for a cold set of rules and fine print that are aimed at one admittedly impressive purpose for existence: profit.

The Bankers could sacrifice their bankerhood for their humanity, or their humanity for their bankerhood, but the two existences do not seem compatible, at least at the same time in a given day. I don't intend to insult them by any means, but I only intend to discover precisely what makes up their essence, their soul, their fundamental nature. And I would be lying if that fundamental nature resembled a human soul made for loving and living in relationship and economy with each other. No, the Banker is not a member of an economy, but a very stumbling block to that shared economy. The Bankers do not want economy- they want monopoly.

Now I know what all the Bankers will tell you. They'll defend themselves with some talk about how they help out people by loaning them money to make their dreams come true when they cannot afford such dreams: a noble purpose for existence, no doubt. But if such nonsense were actually true, why oh why should they charge an interest? I hear you now, Bankers. "What? We're supposed to do it for free? How will we make a living for ourselves?" But I will not denounce usury in its entirety for I admit such a purpose can be useful for the economy of others, but complaining of 'making a living' is quite different than the private jets and porcelain pens your overdraft fees afford you. Agreed? Greed. It has always been the Achilles heel, the fatal hubris, the quintessential vulnerability of the Banker lot.

Furthermore, and in conclusion, could it be possible that the most effective way for a private business to enlist the stronger hand of a public government against a private citizen is the process of loaning vast and irresponsible amounts of money, which is then termed 'debt,' and forcing the stronger hand of the judicial system to seize money from the private citizen, at a profit no less from late fees as from an advanced percentage rate? And then oh then, my friends, to loan so greedily and irresponsibly as to demand from said government billions of dollars in what they quite conspicuously call "bailouts," which of course are paid or at least will be paid by the same private citizens that the Bank hopes to make a profit from in the first place? This is indeed the world we live in, thanks to the heralded and ancient name of Banker.

I must preface with all this, because we are about to enter a bank, friends. And if you thought the world of Artcity quite different, exotic, or whimsical compared to the blah, gray, concrete worlds you know, wait till you see the Bank, any bank for that matter, for the Banker family has spread far and wide, and aren't much different here in Artcity than they are in Lower Manhattan's Financial District.

And so it was on the morning after Vincent's revelation by the Wine Fountain that Vincent and Domino walked along a blue sidewalk towards the Bank of Artcity, owned by Anthony's Corporation of course. It was a vast marble building that looked like a pagan temple in ancient Greece, which is to say of course that it looked a lot like any American capitol building: lots of columns, statues, a dome, the usual stuff. The statues were all famous Bankers: Montagu Norman, Hjalmar Schacht, Emile Moreau, and John Maynard Keynes were most prominent.

At the door, Domino reached for the door handle, but Vincent stopped him. He said, "Wait, we need to have this clear. I'll do all the talking in here- they don't need to know anything about you."

Domino replied, "I said I didn't even want to come. I don't know about this, Mr. Fides."

Vincent said confidently, "No. You're coming in here with me. They want my business. I'm going to take out a huge loan that I'll have to pay interest on. Why wouldn't they want my money?"

Domino shrugged, "My money's not good enough for them."

"Just keep your cool, alright?" Vincent encouraged. "Bankers are a peddler crowd- I understand them. If we walk in as confident businessmen ready to start a business, there's no reason they won't want to go into business with us."

Domino sighed, "Whatever you say, Mr. Fides. I'll keep quiet."

Domino opened the door wide, and gestured his business partner to enter first with kindly respect, saying, "After you."

Vincent smiled, "Thank you, sir."

They both entered the double marble doors and beheld the Bank of Artcity in all its glory. The floor was a mile long, all glass, so you could see the stacks and stacks of gold bars and money stacks that must have been the vault in the basement. The gold bars provided a shine throughout the Bank, a rich saturated gold color emanating upwards from the whole floor. Three hundred customers dashed this way and that, from this desk to that cubicle, from this office to that desk. The ceiling was five stories high with glass chandeliers that would make any nation's queen quite jealous.

Along the immense walls were story-large portraits of the Banker family. And between the portraits were huge scripted quotations.

"Mark Twain: 'A banker is a fellow who lends his umbrella when the sun is shining and wants it back the minute it begins to rain.'"

"Bertold Brecht: 'It is easier to rob by setting up a bank than by holding up a bank clerk.'"

"Thomas Jefferson: 'I sincerely believe that banking establishments are more dangerous than standing armies, and that the principle of spending money to be paid by posterity, under the name of funding, is but swindling futurity on a large scale.'"

Domino leaned over and whispered in Vincent's ear. "I don't understand. They seem proud of being mean."

Vincent shooed him off. "You don't understand Bankers. Let's go."

Vincent led Domino to the colossal main line that seemed to be where the newly arrived were to report. Both Vincent's and Domino's eyes were still wide, looking here and there, very impressed by the whole operation going on around them.

Adjacent to their line was a line of windows where branch Bankers were helping the customers a hundred at a time. Vincent overheard the customer closest: "But I don't understand, Miss. It says 'free' in big letters. Now you're telling me it costs a hundred Clouds. What exactly is 'free' about something that costs a hundred Clouds?"

The Banker responded, "Now you're just being unreasonable, sir. Did you actually expect it to be free?"

The customer shot back, "Yes! I actually did!"

Vincent got to move up a little, so he couldn't hear the rest. The next customer was arguing about an overdraft fee. "It was seven cents!"

The Banker responded calmly, "No, sir. It was five Clouds, twenty-five cents. And then it was seven cents."

The customer realized. "No- Wait. You- You reorganized my transactions- You changed the order, so you could charge me double?! Two overdraft fees!"

The Banker only said, "You really should be more careful with your spending, sir."

"The seven cents wouldn't have cost me thirty-two Clouds if you didn't change the order! Is that even legal?"

The Banker replied, "Well, I didn't do it myself, sir. I assure you of that. If you would like to speak to one of our resident lawyers, you're free to step into that line over there. I'm afraid I've done all I can."

The customer's eyes followed her pointing finger to a line of very grizzly-looking characters, each one looking as if about to throw a boot through a chandelier. He looked back at the Banker, who was already smiling at the next customer. "It'll only be a moment, ma'am. Sir?"

The customer waddled off to the next line, as Vincent and Domino moved further up. The line moved very quickly, like the line at a blood bank, efficiency sucking the volunteers dry before they have a chance to change their minds. Many people griped about this or that, while others walked off with huge grins as if they had just got something for free. It was quite quickly that Vincent and Domino found themselves at a little desk with a young woman.

With a very gentle and soothing voice, she said, "Welcome to the Bank of Artcity, my name's Felicity Banker. How may I assist you?"

Vincent stuttered, "Uh- I'd like to obtain a loan to begin a theatre."

The very gentle and soothing voice replied, "Oh, how delightful. Another theatre for our world. Sounds like a great use of our resources here at the Bank."

Vincent stuttered again, "Yea- Right, I mean- I think so."

Domino jabbed Vincent in the abdomen with a pointy elbow.

Vincent continued with false bravado, "And where should I go? Who should I speak to about our doing business together?"

The young woman looked at her clipboard, made a mark, looked back up at Vincent, and then smiled largely. "I think J.J. can take care of you. He is that young man sitting just there. Thank you so much for visiting us today."

Vincent looked over to a little desk about twenty paces to his right where he saw a very, very young man in a pinstriped, three-piece suit typing on his keyboard. Vincent was a little confused. He looked back at the young woman who already had eye contact with the next customer in line. Vincent interrupted her, "Um, Miss?"

"It's Madame, sir. How can I assist you further?" came the gentle voice.

Vincent stumbled, "Oh, I'm sorry. Madame, um, he kind of looks like a kid- A child I mean."

The young woman smiled dully. "Well he is a kid, sir. But I assure you he is more than capable of taking care of you. I mean, let's be honest, it's just the loan department."

Vincent was still confused after the response, but felt too intimidated to ask any further. So he simply responded, "Yes, of course. Thank you."

Vincent and Domino edged slowly closer and closer to the desk to which they had been appointed. When Vincent and Domino were about halfway, the kid in the three-piece looked up from his computer screen and noticed the nervous customers edging closer and closer to the two unoccupied chairs at his desk. He rolled his eyes, as he had enjoyed the brief moment of relaxation mid-shift without having to deal with the ignorant people that usually decided one fine random day to start a business and realized quite quickly that they would first need to obtain a loan from the Bank.

As they neared, Vincent noticed the huge colorful nameplate that read proudly: J.J. Banker.

J.J. folded his hands on the desk before him and mustered up a smile. "How can I help you guys today?"

Vincent and Domino, standing before the desk, and looking seemingly straight down at the kid, smiled nervously. Vincent said, "Well, I'd like a loan… uh, sir. I'd like to start a theatre."

J.J. rolled his eyes again. "Oh, another theatre. Just what the world needs. Please sit down, and we'll get your paperwork settled."

Vincent and Domino sat down quickly and in unison, like soldiers fresh out of boot camp or Catholics at the Latin Mass. Vincent smiled, "You mean you're going to give me the loan just like that?"

J.J. smiled at their ignorance. "Well, I don't see any reason why not. It's not our place to judge how well your business will do, nor how efficient you are as a businessman. You want money, and we've got it. This is really a very simple industry to understand, believe it or not."

Vincent looked at Domino with a big smile and slapped him playfully on the shoulder. Domino beamed back, thinking about his theatre.

J.J. went back to his keyboard. "Name?"

Vincent leaned back in the chair and put one leg over the other. "Vincent Fides, the peddler of dreams."

J.J. flinched at the sound of the name. He started typing.

Domino was already making his theatre's first season up in his mind. *The Tempest*, definitely, opening production. Then maybe something more modern, *Waiting for Godot*, he thought. Yea, perfect.'

J.J. found the page he was looking for, and kept typing. "Hm, that's interesting."

Vincent was still smiling. "What's that?"

J.J. finished typing. He bit his lip. He folded his hands before him. "I'm sorry, gentlemen, but I can't do anything for you at this time."

Both Vincent's and Domino's triumphant smiles decayed abruptly. Vincent asked loudly, "At this time?"

Domino stood up, "It's cuz I'm painted, isn't it."

J.J. said calmly, "No-... Well, I don't know, actually. I-... I'm sorry. I can't talk about it."

Vincent continued, "What do you mean, you can't talk about it? Why can't I, who am not a clown, have a loan?"

J.J. was getting upset. "What part of 'I can't talk about it' don't you understand?"

Vincent stood up too. "Don't you get smart with me, boy."

J.J. rose from his seat. "Don't call me 'boy,' dork."

Domino slapped Vincent's arm. "Vincent! Stop it- He's like... ten."

J.J. screamed, "And a half, shorty!"

Domino shot back. "Shorty?... Forget this." He reached over the desk and got one grabbing hand on the kid's suit jacket before Vincent held him back, sending J.J. tumbling to the ground on his backside.

J.J. shrugged from the ground, "Don't stop him. What do you got, stubby?"

Domino defended himself. "You're shorter than I am!"

J.J. laughed, "I'm ten!"

Domino screamed, "And a half!"

Vincent ripped Domino away from the desk and dragged the disappointed clown away.

J.J. laughed again as he stood up. "Have to have him to protect you, huh?"

And Vincent led Domino swiftly out of the Bank.

Chapter Thirteen:
The Dark Night

Darkness walked slowly across the Artcity sky. Many people think of day and night as opponents who never meet, but day and night are best friends, complementary, always holding hands as they walk slowly around this little globe, each embracing their little share of our atmosphere. They're never jealous of each other. They never try to move in on each other's territory, trying to expand their own power and influence. They just prance around and around forever. And so the night embraced Anna as she paced her bedroom, wondering how a dream could ever come true for her.

The dark night is perhaps the most misunderstood, the most miscomprehended, the most mysterious of our stations along the Universal way. So many people think the dark night is just about suffering, but suffering is part of the whole human lot- we all must bear it. No, the dark night is something altogether different than bad things happening, no matter how bad. The dark night isn't bad fortune, or the residue of another man's sin- no, the dark night is about the light leaving you behind.

If you are to progress past a generic, shallow experience of life, and enter into true life, which is of its essence without death and therefore immortal, you will have to enter the dark night, and you will have to emerge somehow to a new day, a new dawn. But how do you find hope when there is nothing, absolutely nothing outside of you that provides that hope? How do you muster any courage when every material atom in the universe conspires against you? How do you love in the dark?

As Anna tried hard to find the answers to these Universal questions, Bambina entered with her friend's laundry. When Bambina noticed Anna pacing, she stopped, and said, "Oh, come on, Anna- snap out of it."

Anna played it off. "What? I'm fine."

Bambina chuckled, "Fine, right."

Anna laughed. "Oh, stop it. I'm fine."

Bambina laid down the laundry on Anna's white dresser, and then sat down on the bed. She grew more solemn as she asked, "Do you love him, or is he just a way out of here?"

Anna stumbled at the question. "I'm… I'm taken. Somebody else already owns me."

Bambina smiled. "Anthony owns a piece of paper, Anna. Vincent won't give up on account of a piece of paper."

Anna tried to smile, but couldn't. She sat down beside her friend. "Bambina, I've been wondering, and you don't have to talk about it if you don't want to, but the other day when you spoke so- so knowledgeably about men calling women beautiful, and…"

Bambina's smile faded slowly like the twilight. "You want to know."

Anna continued, "It's just that I'm your best friend, and I- well, I kind of think I might never be the same again if Vincent leaves, and not in a good way."

Bambina lowered her head. There was a pause as Anna knew she couldn't find any better words than what she had just stuttered through.

Bambina smiled gently. "Alright. I suppose it could help you." Her head remained low, staring at the ground as she continued. "I did once love a man. A man so beautiful, and tender, and wise. He was my whole life. He walked with me every day. And spoke to me- He spoke to me in everything. I could hear him plain as day. I heard him screaming out to me from the rolling hills of grass that surround the City. From the deafening ocean roar. From the stars- all the stars at night- they'd shine in unison, like Morris Code, screaming, 'I love you!'"

Anna smiled sympathetically at the thought.

"And he told me that I was beautiful, me. That I was worth all the stars, and all the waves, and every blade of grass- He said I was worth more than it all to him. And I knew- I knew he meant it. I knew that nothing else in the whole universe could provide for him the way I could provide for him. And I knew nothing else, in the whole little universe could ever make me smile but him. He was the only thing that could bring me any joy at all. If I laughed at a funny kid playing on the street, I knew it was because he put that kid there for me. If I felt happiness from anything, from putting on my shoes backwards accidentally or tripping over a shoelace, I knew it was because he was near, playing a little practical joke on me.

"I knew he loved me. So nothing else could ever matter so long as he loved me. I was so safe in his wonderful arms, and the whole universe held me. Every single morning, when I very first awoke, when my eyes first opened, I could hear him. The voice of my Beloved! Behold, he comes, leaping upon the mountains, bounding over the hills. My Beloved is like a gazelle, or a young stag. He raced and raced. And I chased and chased. Always following, forever following, but distantly hand in hand. My Beloved spoke to me, 'Arise, my love, my fair one, and come away; for lo, the winter is past, the rain is over and gone. The flowers appear on the earth, the time of singing has come.' And we sang and sang. And my heart danced and danced."

But Bambina stopped, almost choking on her exhaled breath. Anna looked down at the ground, too. She said very quietly, "But what happened?"

Bambina sighed deeply, trying to regain her breath. When she did, she continued, "Upon my bed one dark night I sought him whom my soul loves; I sought him, but found him not; I called him, but he gave no answer. I said, 'I will rise now and go about the city, in the streets and in the squares; I will seek him whom my soul loves.' I sought him, but found him not. The watchmen found me, as they went about in the city. 'Have you seen him whom my soul loves?' But they did not know of whom I was speaking about [12].... It has been many years since I last heard him, that voice that my very flesh aches to hear. My soul thirsts for him- My flesh faints for him, as in a dry and weary land where no water is.[13] I didn't know why he left me, without a word. But he left. And with him went all my happiness, all my joy, all my smiles, the true ones, the ones that explode from my very soul."

Anna offered, "I'm so sorry, Bambina."

But Bambina continued unimpeded. "But I love him still, Anna! I will always love him. Even when I cannot feel his strong arms holding me, even when I cannot hear that blissful voice, even when the stars stop twinkling, I can't help but love him."

Anna was confused suddenly. "But why, Bambina? He left you. He hurt you."

"No, no, Anna, not at all," Bambina shot back. "He is only testing my love, purifying my love. You see, he needs me to love him for who he is, not for what he can give me, or do for me. When he walked with me every day, I did not see- I was blind. I loved him because of how he made me feel. I had to learn something that I am only now, years later, beginning to understand."

Anna couldn't understand. "What? Why would he leave?"

Bambina smiled softly. "I have to love him simply because he is lovable. I have to love him, him, who he is. And I could only love him truly, fully, when he left me. He will come back soon now. I believe that. Because like everything else in this life, even a dark night must pass."

Anna didn't speak. She had no more words. She just sat there, beside her friend, and watched the ground as the starlight of this night lit her room.

Bambina sat there too, as if in a trance. "He'll come," she said several times in ever quieter tones. "Make haste, my Beloved, and be like a gazelle in rushing back to me."

Elsewhere in the dark night, in the parking lot of the Bank of Artcity, young J.J. Banker was strolling out of work. A slim thief in black arose from the shadows of the trees and pressed a knife in the young Banker's back.

The thief spoke violently, "You'll give me that loan one way or another, Banker!"

And the thief dragged the terrified child back into the bank.

Chapter Fourteen: The Border Scene

Anna didn't recognize that this day was different than any other- that's the way it is with conversions. Now notice most importantly that Anna has been primed for her conversion: she has already been watching ACTV for many years. Conversions can happen in the blink of an eye, a person like Anthony becoming a person like Federico, but such a conversion is indeed rare, and theologically speaking, a debatable violation of free will on the part of the Lord who has the power to change bread into human flesh or big bang a universe into existence. But most times, a conversion takes a lot of work, a lot of time, a lot of development, before it is finally capped off with what they will remember as their "conversion experience."

And even after all this, there is the final and most important stage: the decision to change an old life and forge a new one, which is of course a decision that must be renewed every moment and with every breath of remaining life. Conversions are indeed hard- don't kid yourself. Most of the work is left up to the person who has to seek that which he does not have. That's the way the Lord usually works in human history, with all due respect and encouragement towards free will.

So Anna didn't see the culminating experience on the horizon, even though she had been fermenting for quite a while, passing the earlier stages of conversion unnoticed for years now. As per her usual weekday, she got up, dressed, brushed her teeth, tried to have a conversation with Bambina while swishing the toothpaste bubbles around her mouth (with various levels of success), performed the morning ritual, ate a light breakfast (for what good is a day if it doesn't start with bacon?), and readied herself for her morning walk to Anthony's theatuh for rehearsal. In her moments of solitude, as Bambina bumbled all around her, she went over various lines she was memorizing, Kant, Goethe, Plato.

Any moment now. Any single moment may be just a tock away from the most important in life. That's why everyone has to enjoy life, to truly have fun in life. That's what people really don't understand about the clowns and the Universals. They think it's all 'Do this' and 'Don't do that'- they don't see that for every 'yes' a man chooses, he says 'no' to a million other choices. When a child chooses to become a poet, the child must say 'No' to being an astronomer or an atheist, for those things are completely incompatible with being a poet. So the poet says 'No' to something, but the very basis of saying 'No' is only in order to be free to say 'Yes' to something else. That is the choice that everyone must make a thousand times a day. 'No' to a taco, and 'Yes' to a tamale. 'No' to the salsa verde, and 'Yes' to the red. 'No' to the chicken, but 'Yes' to the pig. And that's just lunch.

Everyone must be ready every moment of every day, even Mondays- because the moment of surprise, that split second that he realizes something he's never realized before could come at any tock. So have 'Yes' on your lips, and a 'No' in your pocket- give 'em out as they're deserved.

The very moment Anna opened her front door, there came a very loud, and very, very beautiful (if I may say so myself) concertina chanting her along. She walked to the chant like a snake dances to one of those eastern flutes, conscious of something new guiding her but unable to change or stop or refuse what she knew she wanted.

Anna walked her usual first two blocks to the theatuh, immediately noticing that the customary traffic of walkers and drivers and bicycles and unicycles and horse carts and trolleys were all gone- there wasn't a soul on the streets but hers.

There's a certain loneliness that every convert must go through. It's a fog, a sitting cloud- I think it was once called a Cloud of Unknowing. What happens is the convert doesn't really fit in with the old people anymore, but he doesn't really know the new people yet. Or, put another way, he can't understand the people he's always understood, but that new knowledge only makes him aware of how distant he is from what he does want. And so there's a certain cloud of solitude the convert must pass through, as the Sculptor gently forms and shapes all of his consents into a new life.

The streets were still empty as she approached her first turn, surprised to find a huge orange sign that read, "DETOUR. This way to the theatuh is closed for renovation by order of your Dad. Follow the signs." And there was a very large arrow pointing right (she would usually make a left). She shrugged innocently and followed the arrow, still unsuspecting of her entire life taking on a new course with her new arrow.

The moment she was on the new street she found another orange sign. "You are finally on the right path." She giggled at the thought of being on the right path. She felt somewhat excited suddenly, as anyone who is devoted to a routine feels while breaking that routine, like a kid missing school or a writer missing a deadline. That sort of dangerous, uncomfortable, but somehow exhilarating feeling of doing something, being something… new.

She was beginning to understand that this day was for something special, that something or someone wanted more from her today. She didn't concentrate on her every step and breath, but she knew that something or someone was guiding her away from her routine, her old way, and by definition, into a new way.

As she walked, she noticed a very large red carpet ahead, smack dab in the middle of the street. Thinking the red carpet for someone else, she went to the side of the street. But just as she swayed away from the red carpet, the Sage of Rustici Palace appeared seemingly out of thin air, and bumped her waist with his, moving her right onto the red carpet. The moment of the clumsy bump brought a haunting violin into the sonata of the religious concertina. As she looked confusedly at the Sage, she wandered to the other side of the carpet, but just as her feet left the red, the smiling, bearded, olive-skinned troubadour they call Luce (a tip of my boater hat) screamed a lyric to the chanting concertina as he appeared beside her.

"Some sweet sound calls you,
Enchanting and alluring.
There's no escape now,
Enchanting and enduring.
Some sweet sound names you,
Whisp'ring of devotion.
You smile discreetly,
New life set in motion.
I'm yours! All yours!
Take me, but be tender.
I'm scarred, all scarred!
But I surrender.
Accept me.
I won't look back.
I'm yours! All yours!
Ravish me, Love, attack!"

Anna jumped at the booming tenor in her ear, and consequently jumped right back on the red carpet. And so Anna was escorted down the red carpet, flanked by the Sage and Luce. Anna watched as dozens of people, clowns, artists, children appeared on balconies above both sides of the street. She walked slowly, in awe, as they all showered the street with red and white roses.

And just as Anna finally thought, 'What is this?', she approached the gargantuan, frescoed sign that read, "Thank you for coming to Artcity! ... Where fairytales come true." Just beyond, about ten more paces, a tiny wooden sign read, "Clown Town." Anna was immediately uncomfortable. She looked at the two gentlemen escorting her, to the balconies, and then forward to Clown Town.

The red carpet ended at the thick painted line that marked the border, and the two men stopped as she approached it. The singing had stopped. The combo of violin and concertina chanted softer, and softer. She looked ahead into a filthy, dark, and misty neighborhood, the night to Artcity's day. She looked at the two gentlemen one last time- they both smiled and nodded, tipping hats to the miss, before turning and walking away, their music following them, fainter, and fainter.

Anna faced Clown Town, the last haven of true art, and true life, in the ancient and lauded Artcity. After three moments to take in the picture, she suddenly recognized the clown security guard from the theatuh who was fired the week before. She ran over to her.

"Gelsomina!" Anna called, happy to have found a familiar face in unfamiliar territory.

Gelsomina sat on a pile of trash bags on the sidewalk, reading studiously an old beaten copy of Ratzinger's *Called to Communion* with huge, oversized reading glasses. "Ooo-Anna! How odd to find you here," Gelsomina exclaimed, obviously faking surprise.

Anna said unsurely, "Well, I- I think I'm on a detour. I was headed to the theatre."

Gelsomina smiled, "Oh, it's just up there."

Anna looked down the long Clown Town street. "I'm a little confused."

Gelsomina only smiled bigger. "Have you ever been to Clown Town?"

"No," Anna replied. "My Dad would never let me."

Gelsomina said proudly, "Oh, it's a great place. It's how Artcity used to be."

"I've actually heard that before," Anna said, as indeed Bambina had often talked about her Clown Town home.

Anna continued awkwardly, "Hey, I'm sorry about your losing your job and everything."

Gelsomina waved her off nonchalantly. "It's okay. Sir Anthony's a prick anyway."

Anna thought it over, then nodded. "I've never heard it articulated so well."

Gelsomina smiled again. "Thank you!"

Anna looked back down the long dark street. "Um, do you wanna come with me to the theatre, at least show me where it is?"

Gelsomina closed her book and stood up. "Of course. That's why I was here waiting for you. I love Domino's art- he really is brilliant."

Anna forced a smile. "Domino? He's... at the theatre?"

Gelsomina smacked her shoulder rather hard, but playfully. "Well sure he's there. He owns it!" Gelsomina started walking along the sidewalk, as Anna gazed after her.

"Oh. Of course," Anna said slowly.

Anna looked back toward the bright skyline of Artcity, realizing finally in totality that she's headed for a very different theatre. She nodded her head with a small smile, making her free will, abandoning Anthony's Artcity for Vincent's Clown Town.

She jogged to catch up to Gelsomina who hadn't waited for her free will. Anna laughed, "The world may end soon, so I suppose I should have some fun first."

Gelsomina scoffed, "Why do they do that anyway?"

Anna asked, "Do what?"

Gelsomina continued, "Try to predict the end of the world. If the end of the world does come when they say it will, no one will be around to congratulate them on their guess, and if it doesn't happen, everyone will be around to make fun of them for being wrong. I just mean that it would make much more sense to predict a date that the end of the world will *not* happen. Then, if it does end, nobody can scold you. And if the world continues, everyone will call you a genius."

Gelsomina made a turn down a dark alley, Anna trying to keep up as much with Gelsomina's scurrying feet as her scurrying lips. Gelsomina concluded, "Might as well be a meteorologist is all: the pay's better."

In the dark alley, they found a final large orange sign. "Turn right, Anna," the sign read in huge block letters. Anna looked sharply at Gelsomina, seeing her name, but Gelsomina only smiled and nodded as if to say, 'I told you so.'

Gelsomina disappeared into the dark alley, as Anna stared at the orange sign. She finally smiled, realizing the campaign that had brought her here. And she proceeded, disappearing down the dark alley, too.

Now it's fair to ask what happened differently today, other than a few big orange signs. But a lot of people seem to think conversions are some kind of miraculous and supernatural experience. They can be, of course, as there are most certainly things that science doesn't know how to explain, like the kingly wounds appearing on certain followers without forceful insertion for instance. But by far most conversions are far more subtle, like human life itself. You see, if this Universal Way is indeed the only true humanism, which I most certainly contend with and without my concertina (I sing it on the mountaintops, I mean), then genuine experience of the Lord need not be at *His* plane of reality but at *ours*, for He Himself came down to ours. He reaches for us far more efficiently than we reach for Him, so religious experience must then be identifiable with *our* lives, *our* existences, even amidst the normal humdrum of a routinely lived day. The Lord is always there, sometimes with huge orange signs in His huge sheltering hands. But by far most times, He gets one of His friends to hold the signs for Him. It's simply the way the Old Guy likes to work, you see.

CHAPTER FIFTEEN:
A SERENADE

As Anna turned the dark corner to follow Gelsomina, she immediately and clumsily bumped into a thick wooden signpost. As she recovered from the collision, she read it: "Domino's Universal Theatre" was hand-painted in thick red letters. The alley opened up into what appeared to be a backyard. There was a crowd gathered around a huge wooden box. The show just happened to be starting.

The curtains flew open to reveal a puppet with the back of her hand on her forehead. Domino shouted in his exaggerated female voice, "O, woe is me! I'm the princess of a great city but that I art only brings me trouble. I have to do this and that just to please everyone!"

Vincent slapped a boy puppet down. In his deepest voice, he said proudly, "Hello, miss! How are you this beautiful dark night?"

"Ooo, you frightened me," Domino replied in his high voice. "Oh. Who are you?"

Vincent's puppet extended a hand. "Vincent Fides, the peddler of dreams, at your service. And you are?"

A crowd member wondered aloud, "Who's Vincent?"

Domino continued, "I'm Anna, Princess, actress, dancer, singer- I play the harp and the trumpet, I'm a sculptor- Well, I consider myself a-"

Vincent slapped Domino's back, making both puppets shake. Vincent continued in his deep voice, "It's wonderful to meet you, Anna."

The same crowd member wondered aloud again. "Anna?"

Anna watched with a small smile, judging her portrayal.

Domino's girl puppet responded, "Oh you, too. But- Well, you should probly leave now or the evil owner of... (in his normal voice)... the Corporation..."

Domino waited as the audience hissed and howled with glee at the sound of the Corporation.

When the applause died down, he continued, "...will come and take me away from you."

Vincent's puppet slapped the air with his hand. "Oh, I'm not afraid of some rich businessman dork."

Domino said loudly, "I'm supposed to marry him, though. My father says I have to."

"Let me convince your father that I'm the man you should marry," Vincent replied.

Domino's puppet jumped at Vincent's. "Oh I love thee, Vincent Fides, peddler of dreams!"

Vincent shook away. In his normal voice, he said, "Stop it. Stop it, Domino!"

Domino gathered himself again. "Oh. Yes. Sorry." Then he said louder so Anna could hear him, "Sorry, Anna."

Anna was already smiling largely. "It's quite alright, Domino," she called back to him.

The curious crowd member finally had had enough. He lunged forward, interrupting the play, "This is supposed to be Romeo & Juliet. Who is this Vincent, Domino? What's going on here?"

Gelsomina slapped him violently with her program. "Let him run his theatre!"

The crowd member ducked out of the way. "I just wanna know who Vincent is!"

Vincent appeared at the side of the stage with a hand raised. "Um, I'm Vincent."

Gelsomina pointed for the crowd member, "He's Vincent."

The crowd member asked again, "Who are you?"

Gelsomina said obviously, "He just said he's Vincent."

Vincent said, "Vincent."

But the crowd member's confusion remained. "So it's Vincent and Juliet?"

Vincent laughed. "No, it's Vincent and Anna!"

The crowd member asked exhaustedly, "Who's Anna?"

Anna, who was standing just beside the man in complete enjoyment, raised her hand. "I'm Anna."

The crowd member jumped, his feet actually leaving the ground, in fear. "Who are you?"

Gelsomina said to Anna, "Don't answer that."

The crowd member looked around, then stormed off. "I'm leaving! I can't take this anymore! I'm tired already, and this is only the first act!"

The play continued with Vincent constantly surprising Anna everywhere she went, to her loud delight, as played by Domino.

At some point, Anna began asking Gelsomina random questions about Domino's theatre, but she was trying to concentrate on the great art before her. After two acts of interruptions, Gelsomina was livid. "Ssh!"

The dozen nearest crowd members hissed, "Sh!"

Anna jumped at the sound, frightened to death. She looked at her feet, embarrassed, as various theatre patrons (ah, the theatre patrons) shook their heads in unison with the disgust of broken protocol.

Domino was slightly disturbed by the fuss in the audience, but as any professional, kept going.

At the end, the small curtains flew closed, and Domino and Vincent appeared on either side of the small stage, bowing together to wild applause from their audience, the wildest of course coming from Gelsomina who whistled and howled with praise. Each of Domino's hands pulled red roses out of thin air mid-bow, nonchalantly tossing them to his fans.

The crowd dispersed, lingering around the backyard. Vincent went directly to Anna. "How was it?" he asked gingerly.

"It was entertaining."

"How are you?"

"As good as, um, a princess could be," Anna replied with a sarcastic grin.

Vincent laughed. "You could renounce your throne."

But Anna's smile faded slightly.

Vincent said quickly, "I know, I know. How about a walk?"

Anna nodded. And they wondered off together down the alley.

Meanwhile, Gelsomina had gone directly to Domino. "Ooo, Domino, it was wonderful! Just wonderful- You're so talented."

Domino bowed again, "Grazie, grazie."

After an awkward pause of Gelsomina tapping her foot on the ground, she said shyly, "So, um, do you need any help cleaning up?"

Domino looked at his admirer with a bent head, like a curious dog examining something he's never noticed before. After torturing her a bit with biting his lip and looking her up and down, he smiled. "I suppose so." As the two wondered over to the little theatre to begin folding curtains, Domino shook his head. "You're like mice or facial hair- you just keep coming back." They began working, Gelsomina's eyes glued to her man, her man pretending not to notice.

Elsewhere in the world, Anthony Ceo paced in front of the Theatuh d'Artcity. He looked down the street several times, glanced at his watch, and finally reentered the theatuh in a hurry.

On a dark street in Clown Town, Vincent stared at Anna's hand but never made a move. They walked calmly along the foggy road, a patient pace, looking around at the Clown Town scenery.

Finally, Vincent found a question. "How's the show goin'?"

"Anthony closed down the production," Anna said. "You didn't hear?"

Vincent made his usual confused face. "How come? He was obsessed with that thing."

Anna tried to be subtle. "He won't say. I wouldn't doubt if my Dad had something to do with it, though."

Vincent was still confused. "Cuz of the clowns?"

Anna's subtlety wore off. "My Dad doesn't care about the clowns."

Vincent realized that he was the reason. He silently said, "Oh."

After a few more patient steps, Anna continued. "We were still supposed to rehearse today. It's been nice without Anthony around so much. I'd like to act for once without him breathing down my neck."

Vincent laughed. "Just wait. Domino's going to open a theatre in Artcity. It'll be perfect for you."

Anna joked, "I don't know if his costumes will fit me."

It took a moment for Vincent to get the joke, because it wasn't very funny. After a few more patient steps, Vincent stopped. "So I've been thinking about our predicament here."

But Anna didn't stop, and kept strolling slowly. "Which part?"

"I've thought about this a long time," Vincent began. "And it's really just your Dad and Anthony standing in our way. And your Dad probably just thinks I'm some piece of junk who's not worthy of his daughter, but I bet no one would ever live up to his expectations, right?"

Anna nodded calmly.

Vincent continued, "Then all I've gotta do is prove myself to him."

Anna asked quietly, "And Anthony and the contract?"

Vincent shook his head. "Why did your Dad ever sign that thing?"

"It was Congressman Scottie Johnson. He made a deal with Anthony for Daddy's campaign funding."

"But why did your Dad ever sign it?"

Anna said, "Oh. Well, Scottie just slipped it into the health care reform as an earmark. Daddy didn't read the whole thing, so he didn't realize till the newspapers published it the next day. He signs a lot of stuff every day, you see. He can't read two-thousand pages every day."

"So marrying the head of the corporation was a matter of state health care reform? That's a little depressing," Vincent joked.

"Tell me about it," Anna laughed. "You have no idea how many kindergarten ideas get slipped into legislation."

"How do we get out of it?" Vincent asked.

"Daddy's been trying for two years," Anna said. "It's on record as public policy."

Vincent replied, "I'm not the most avid political watcher, but I don't get it. Your Dad's the Mayor- Why doesn't he just say, 'Hey, they slipped this stupid thing in here, but it doesn't belong here, so forget it.' I mean, he just doesn't have to honor it."

"But politicians are policy-makers- that's their job," Anna answered. "So we have policies and ways that things are done. To betray the very process that unites us is to set a precedent for chaos and anarchy. We can't start using special circumstances and conditional laws, like 'No stealing... unless you need dinner.' That's criminal."

Vincent laughed. "That's just what politicians use to explain away their ineptitude and ineffectiveness in actually representing or helping the people. They invent a process and then abuse that process by representing not the people, but special interests, such as the political party that assisted them in obtaining a place of leadership in the first place. Then they excuse their corruption by saying, 'This is the way it's always done'? That's ridiculous. How does anything ever get done?"

Anna chuckled.

Vincent continued, "We devote ourselves to this side with all our strength, until we realize how ignorant, narrow, and dangerous that party's vision would be for our nation. And so we vote them all out of office and devote ourselves completely to their sworn enemies, until they mess up because they represent their own platform instead of our national interest. And so we switch back, and back again, in a seemingly endless cycle of campaign and election. Sounds like clinical schizophrenia to me."

Anna laughed, and they walked along for a while as a brisk dusk began walking along the sky. Vincent didn't have a jacket to give Anna, so he didn't bother. Anna still enjoyed her first trip to Clown Town, and thought that though it may be obviously old and worn down from many decades of decay, it was extraordinarily beautiful. She had found a time warp to another age, when carpentry and construction actually mattered to people, as opposed to the three-quarter siding of various dull earth tones that dominated her suburbanized Artcity. And even though she didn't feel quite safe in this dark place, she loved Clown Town and felt more alive than she had ever felt before.

It wasn't long, however, before both minds returned to the problems that separated them. And both minds knew there was much more than a silly earmark standing in their way.

Anna thought it was a matter of how things are and have to be, the powers that rule her life subjecting her will to theirs, and so her hope for a better life was dwindling far below Vincent's. She didn't feel powerless, mind you-what modern woman would? Just trapped. And what modern woman wouldn't?

Vincent meanwhile thought the same thought that had persecuted him since the moment he got to Artcity: 'What oh what do you offer a people that have everything already?' He knew the only answer to their problems: he would have to somehow find his peddlerhood again, not in order to sell empty promises and guileless guarantees, like the politicians. Nope. Vincent knew he would have to find some new dreams to pass out. He thought of Domino's theatre, of all the clowns, even of Anna's father, who just wanted a good man for his beloved daughter. And for the first time, he realized that the great and lauded Artcity actually needed him.

Still silent, Vincent and Anna journeyed into a park, walking toward an old fountain with as many cracks as stars in the sky. A huge statue of one of the nymphs or furies stood proudly atop the fountain, looking down on the two. In the far distance, Anna saw that famous troubadour, Luce, standing atop a picnic table with his concertina. Vincent flinched as he heard what sounded like a record player, the loud crackling echoing throughout the park. He didn't notice Domino and Gelsomina sneak behind them and hide behind a tree, Gelsomina with an amp pointed towards the lovers, Domino making a crackling noise into a microphone that sounded like old vinyl on a record player. Luce began belting out his powerful tenor.

As the music began, Vincent smiled awkwardly at Anna, and extended his hands. "Ready to teach me?" She smiled, and they danced.

Beloved,
The very ground below you
Is weakening to the touch-
Your soft heels ascending mid-air.
The cool wind is blowing,
Your stockings showing.
Something's pulling you skyward
While old Gravity sleeps unaware.

Beloved,
We're racing by the stars now,
Pulled by the scream screaming
'Today, today, today!'
Joined at the hands,
And helpless to demands.
This force has got us,
Trapped to flying away.

But could this be love, dear?
I know nothing of this above, dear.
I don't understand,
But give me your hand.
I'm not falling for you,
I'm rising fear for fear.

So beloved,
I cannot feel the hours move,
But tell me what is this power trying to prove?
I'll unplug these stars
If you give me your scars,
And scream back, 'I love you!'

While the two danced, they never noticed Chief
Petrarch and Deputy Peire d'Alvernhe appear at the park's
entrance, walking straight towards Vincent with handcuffs
already drawn. Domino saw them in the distance, and ran
up to intercept them. Gelsomina reluctantly took over the
crackling sound, as she watched Domino ask the police
officers various questions, the Chief pointing at Vincent in
response. Domino looked back to the dancers, smiled, and
turned back to the officers. Domino told the Chief
something that obviously surprised him. The Chief
reluctantly placed the handcuffs on Domino, and led him
away.

Vincent and Anna danced and danced as the night came to join them, a certain concertina providing the rhythm beat for falling in love, oblivious to mayors or ceos or cops or robbers, or the sacrifice that a good friend made for them to dance on into the night.

CHAPTER SIXTEEN:
THE OLD CONVENTION
OF MISTAKEN IDENTITY

As morning came, Vincent and Anna walked with purpose back to the Bank of Artcity. Vincent hoped that having the Mayor's daughter on his arm might help Domino's situation. It was Anna's idea, of course, as Vincent would never suggest a thing such as using Anna's power and prestige as a tool for advancement. Anna didn't like to throw her name around much, but for Domino and Vincent, she was more than obliged to make an exception, especially as concerned the Bank- she missed Pangaea too.

As they walked along the sidewalk, Vincent was telling Anna how odd it was for Domino to disappear. Vincent had walked Anna home before returning to Domino's Clown Town theatre, but neither Domino nor Gelsomina were there. Vincent hadn't been alone since the first day he had arrived in Artcity and met his new friend. Anna wasn't quite sure how concerned she should be. Clowns are kind of notorious for being spontaneous and impulsive and unplanned and unstructured, which usually drives organized people crazy (stage managers in particular). She hoped that her favorite foreigner was simply overreacting. 'Maybe Domino and Gelsomina wanted some privacy too,' she thought.

Nevertheless, as they approached the Bank of Artcity, their minds were refocused on the project at hand: getting a loan for Domino's theatre, vis-à-vis Vincent's deal. Vincent opened the big, heavy door of the Bank for his lady, and they entered.

Immediately, Vincent was surprised to find not half of the people hustling-bustling around the Bank that he had seen the other day. The Bank was nearly empty. The second thing Vincent noticed was that all the gold bars below the glass floor, and the glow they had provided, were gone. The Bank seemed more like the white walls of an asylum, if you have ever heard of asylums before, cold and damp, dark and dirty white.

Vincent led Anna to the entrance line, which had only a few people waiting to meet the gentle, young woman at the main desk. In seconds, they reached her.

"Welcome to the Bank of Artcity. How may I assist you?" said the gentle and soothing voice.

Vincent asked, "What happened to everybody?"

"You didn't hear?" Felicity asked, scandalized. "The Bank was robbed just two nights ago. And since there is no money here, we've closed down most of the departments while the government prints off some more money for us."

Vincent scratched his head at the conspicuous admission spoken without a touch of ethical remorse or embarrassment. Anna didn't even flinch, conditioned as she was to expect such nonsense as realism.

"You don't say," Anna said, frightened. "Did they catch the culprit yet?"

"Yes, they did, thank Medici," Felicity replied. "Just last night, they apprehended him."

Vincent leaned in. "Well, we're here for a loan."

Felicity's gentle smile returned. "Oh, the loan department is still open, of course. No sense closing that one down, right? I think J.J. can help you again- he helped you the other day, right? Only do please be gentle with him. He was the one the robber held at knifepoint."

With a sympathetic nod to the young woman, Anna turned to face young J.J. Banker who was busily typing at his computer. She walked over to him, Vincent hiding somewhat behind her, unsure of how J.J. would react to his return, especially with the Mayor's daughter and all. Anna noticed Vincent seeming to hide behind him, so she slapped his arm. "What's wrong with you, Vincent?"

Vincent smirked, refusing to answer.

Anna giggled. "He's a child."

Vincent whispered to himself, "Yes, I know how old he is." Vincent again thought of how much he needed this loan, not just to satisfy his debt to Domino but because he genuinely cared about his clown friend now.

As they approached, J.J. looked up and smiled at the approaching Anna, welcoming her to the chair. Before Anna had a chance to respond, Vincent decisively stepped out from behind Anna and plopped down in the chair. "How's it going there, J.J.?"

But J.J. nearly jumped out of his seat, scared to death of seeing Vincent. "What are you doing here?" he said nervously and quickly.

"Well, I really do need that loan, you see," Vincent said. "I don't know what all happened the other day, but for anything I said that might have offended you, I am truly sorry."

Anna was confused both by J.J.'s reaction to seeing her Vincent and Vincent's response.

"What happened the other day is you robbed me, the whole bank! Two days ago, all our gold bars, gone!" J.J. was frantic as he stood up.

"I what?" Vincent asked calmly.

"But I- I thought you were in jail," J.J. said.

Anna chimed in. "You were in jail, Vincent?"

"What? No," Vincent responded. "I didn't rob the bank two days ago. I mean- I've never robbed a bank!"

"You robbed me! Security!" J.J. yelled.

Vincent pointed at Anna with a question mark on his face, but Anna slapped his hand away. Anna said calmly, "Now, look, just calm down a minute. Let's talk about this."

"But the Chief said the robber was arrested last night," J.J. said, trying to calm himself. "He's in custody."

Vincent pointed, "See, then it couldn't have been me."

Anna asked, "What did the Chief say? Who was it?"

J.J. sat back down, trying to gather himself. "I just heard that he caught the robber in a little park on the edge of Clown Town... for loitering. I don't know who it was. I thought it was the peddler." J.J. motioned to Vincent, still visibly shaking.

Vincent stood up. "Let's go, Anna. We'll do this another day."

Anna began to follow Vincent out, but Vincent turned back. "I'll be back for that loan," he said directly with a pointing finger.

J.J.'s hands shot up in the air for a stickup.

Anna smacked him. "Vincent!"

Vincent turned again to leave. "I didn't rob the stupid bank!"

On the way out, Vincent noticed a newspaper stand at the entrance. Plastered on the front page was a colorful mug-shot of his friend Domino. He stopped in his tracks, Anna barreling into him. He picked it up, and sighed, showing it to Anna. Beside the story of Domino's capture was another headline that caught Vincent's eye: 'Federico's Secret-Revealing Speech to Air on ACTV.' Vincent pulled two quarters out of his pocket, dropped them on the floor, and dashed off.

Chapter Seventeen:
The Memorare

In a pristine jail cell, Domino practiced little magic tricks with his deck of cards. Domino made a great sacrifice for his friend Vincent, but he wasn't particularly proud of himself for doing it. His sacrifice was logical: he knew very well that Vincent didn't rob the bank, and it would be better for the exposure of Vincent's framing if Vincent were free. So Domino went to jail in his stead, without any sense of remorse or accomplishment.

Chief Petrarch was at his desk nearby, rereading the newspaper article about Federico's big speech tonight. An old television was on but muted, as the general hoopla, hype, and commentary paraded before the speech. Chief Petrarch was fascinated by Federico. He knew the clowns' argument very well, and also knew the baseless and untenable arguments that Anthony had used to infect Artcity. Chief Petrarch was a clown himself by heritage, but his clownhood simply didn't show. When he was much younger, he had written incredible poetry that set the world aflame, poetry in fact that was still and would be for centuries yet the very standard not only of poets, but of lovers. Many of the world's ideas of love came from his own youthful explorations of his favorite topic.

As age set in, though, Chief Petrarch felt more and more attracted to his clown heritage. He had never really rejected his identity, as others had, but it was simply the case that because he had gained such renown for his youthful love poetry, people could not see the real, and full, poet he had matured into. His new literary pursuits were far more scholarly and explorative than the child he was when he cried to the heavens for a girl he knew he could never have. His new literary passion was the universal pursuit of that most elusive of characters in his life: himself. He thought that without understanding himself, he would be ill-equipped and simply unqualified to help anyone else in their own journeys of life. And so he was a new man, far greater than the young love poet, influential though he was- No, now he was a gallant, a giant, a legend. He was the father of humanism, and the father of a new renaissance of universal thought and exploration.

Federico made far more sense to him than Anthony. He knew plainly, as any thinking man would with common sense, that where Federico appealed to his human reason and human potential, Anthony only appealed to his preconceived loyalties and emotions. Anthony was a mere demagogue, who has his day in the sun, but precisely because of his futility in actually providing any change or progress as he calls it, as is promised by any demagogue worth his salt, posterity will have no recollection nor concern for him in but a moment's time. If you appeal to emotions, you see, and the emotions pass (as all emotions do), then so does your significance in their lives. No, Chief Petrarch needed nothing Anthony had to sell, but was intent as a thinking man to face the truth, Old Veritas, no matter of the consequences to his emotions.

So when Chief Petrarch had first read the day's headline, telling of Federico's Secret-Revealing Speech, he was immediately excited. He thought just maybe, his beloved Artcity might 'progress' from an adolescent emotionalism built on cognitive dissonance to a true Age of Reason, where the true potential of the powerful human spirit can finally rule a popular culture. He believed in that dream, and fought for it every day, albeit instead of with a sword and shield, with a mind and ink.

After rereading the article, Chief Petrarch looked over at his inmate who was making cards disappear with big, waving hands. The Chief asked, "You excited to hear Federico's big speech tonight? I'll turn the volume up."

Domino was still concentrating on his trick. "I've heard him speak before, lots of times."

The Chief said, "Yea, but he's supposed to have some dirt on Anthony. Could mean all the difference for the clowns."

"I already know the secret."

The Chief was intrigued. "Really? Then what's the big secret?"

Domino still concentrated hard on getting his big, waving hands to cuff the card. "Federico's gonna tell you the secret."

The Chief was confused. "Right, but if you already know, why wait for him to tell me?"

Domino was getting annoyed. "You guys are so impatient. He's about to tell you- That's why they're televising the speech, so you can hear the big secret."

Chief Petrarch laughed. "And you're right here."

Domino said triumphantly, "Exactly."

The Chief was confused again. "What do you mean, exactly?"

Domino sighed. "I'm here, in jail, and I'm certainly not here in order to tell you Anthony's secret."

The Chief understood. He rolled his eyes and turned down the volume on the television just loud enough so he and he alone could hear it. Domino went back to his tricks.

After a moment, the front door opened, and Deputy Peire d'Alvernhe escorted a handcuffed Jaded Summers, ACCLU, into the jail. The Chief turned nonchalantly, unsurprised, and then returned his gaze to the television.

Deputy Peire said, "Heya, Chief. Ms. Summers here was loitering near Rustici Palace."

Jaded Summers said calmly, "It's my place of business."

Deputy Peire took the handcuffs off her, and placed her into a cell adjacent to Domino, who sighed with annoyance at the intrusion.

The Chief said over his shoulder, "Good to see ya, Ms. Summers. We'll just place ya in here for a little while... let ya settle down a bit."

Jaded stood at her cell bars, and calmly replied, "I am settle, Chief. I'm simply pointing out that one can't loiter at her own place of business."

The Chief shooed her with a wave of his hand, trying to concentrate on the television. "Save it for the judge, Summers. I don't care."

Deputy Peire returned to the front door. "I'm headin' back out. Have a good one."

Jaded Summers stood at her cell bars, looking out at the Chief and his television. She could feel Domino's gaze, so she reluctantly looked over to him.

Domino was smiling largely. "I told you you were a criminal."

"First of all, you said I was a thief and a hypocrite. They got me for loitering, not-... Second of all, you're here, too. How much of a hypocrite would it make you to call a fellow inmate a 'criminal'?"

Domino couldn't make the paint of his large smile fall a bit. "Doesn't make me a hypocrite to state a fact. You are indeed a criminal."

Jaded looked away, and journeyed back in her cell to the steel bench, and plopped down.

On the television, Federico was being introduced to the microphone with great applause. Anthony Ceo had a long history of frustration with ACTV. He had tried to purchase the television station a dozen times, but some things in this world, believe it or not, are not for sale. The founder and president of ACTV was a beautiful woman whom everyone lovingly called Mother (Come to think of it, I don't even remember her real name. Physically, she was cloistered like me, and like me, her spirit roamed far outside the walls of her cloister, inspiring everyone who would only think of her).

Federico waved his hands a few times, and began, "Thank you, thank you. Thank you, ladies and gentlemen. Brothers and sisters. I first want to thank you all for coming out tonight. A special thank you too to Mother, president of the Network, for getting this into all the homes of those who couldn't be here tonight, whether they're clown supporters or persecutors. We have a lot to get through tonight, so I'll ask for your patience with me.

"It seems that the present generation has done an incredible job of forgetting what Artcity is, why it was founded, and- most importantly- what it used to stand for. I want to take this opportunity first then to tell the kids about our great city- It seems the logical place to begin tonight. We certainly can't talk about what the Corporation has become until we understand why it was formed in the first place.

"Artcity was founded 230 years ago by a group of traveling artists. They wanted a place to call home, and, in their travels, fell in love with our surrounding hills. So they took what money they had saved and slowly began building houses. There are many letters our library still has that report how dissatisfied they were with neighboring towns and cities. They complained that those places were too concerned with power, money, greed in all its forms. And obviously artists don't mean much to businessmen, except perhaps an opportunity to steal a buck or two.

"So the artists started their own city, their own place. Money didn't mean much to these people. Without caring about money, they were free to be artists, to create and perform, to share with each other their unique visions of what this life should be about. All day, every day, they painted, made music together, wrote poetry, danced, and on and on. Can you even imagine such a place, kids? I would guess you can't... And I know it's because of what that City has become.

"Artcity these days has become our founders' worst nightmare. A place of jobs, of businesses governed by a time clock, of a selfish, greedy generation of power-hungry lunatics. I can't fully explain how it happened, how such an incredible world could be flipped upside down in a matter of years. I can't explain it to you, because, in order to, we'd have to understand the mind of a lunatic, the demented ideas of one man that led the charge to the glorification of dusty bank accounts."

Meanwhile, as Chief Petrarch was glued to his television, as Jaded Summers, ACCLU, listened over his shoulder with suspicious interest, and as Domino threw various cards into the air juggling, Vincent Fides, Anna, and Gelsomina approached the back of the jail in the dark night.

Vincent stealthily glanced in the window of Jaded Summers' jail cell. He looked at Anna and Gelsomina, and whispered, "Domino has a guest with him."

Anna said, "Now what, genius?"

Vincent pawed his chin. After a moment, Gelsomina chimed in, "Well? Come on, my Domino's in there."

Vincent said, "I'm thinking, Gelsomina."

Anna chuckled. "Don't you have a jail key in your dreambag?"

Vincent shrugged. "All sold out."

Anna looked down. "We don't have a prayer."

Vincent found his revelation. "What did you say?"

"I said we don't have a prayer."

Vincent laughed. "Perfect. I hope she'll give me one."

Gelsomina was on her tippy-toes. "Well? What do we do?"

Anna said, "You want to let us in on your plan, here, sweetheart?"

Vincent faced the roof of the jail, as the girls stood back, looking at each other with confusion. Vincent whispered loudly,

"Fairest thou where all are fair!

Plead with Christ our sins to spare!"

Mary shifted in her sleep. Her voice muffled by the blanket that covered her, she asked, "Name?"

Vincent responded, "Vincent Fides, the peddler of dreams!"

After a pause, a key flew over the edge of the roof, Vincent catching it mid-flight. Mary quickly wrapped her covers over herself and returned to sleep.

Anna and Gelsomina were stunned, still looking up. Vincent began walking to the front of the jail.

In the meantime, Chief Petrarch was still watching the television intently.

Federico continued, "On his 18th birthday, Anthony Ceo seized control of the Corporation. Now the Corporation has existed since Artcity's founding. The purpose was to collect, distribute, and support the arts and artists of this City. Our City not only existed on exports, we thrived on them. Within decades, every city in the region turned to Artcity for stimulation, encouragement, entertainment, decoration, and guidance. Soon towers were erected, monuments, stadiums- Soon Artcity went from a little town to a thriving metropolis.

"But then Anthony took over. Now in the very idea of a corporation, with thousands of different people performing thousands of different tasks, it's very difficult to know what is going on at every phase of production. No one has known or even questioned the authority of the Corporation because of its history. And that is why when Anthony was proclaimed owner and Ceo of the Corporation, no one even knew to ask questions. One of the great failures of our society is our consistently pathetic attempts to truly police corporate crime, and this is the crime that has far longer arms than the petty street crook's."

As Domino tried a new magic trick, Jaded Summers journeyed over to his cell, evaluating him. "I can help you with that one. It's really easy."

Domino scoffed, "You don't believe in magic."

Jaded laughed. "I don't believe in someone else's magic. I believe in myself."

"Shouldn't you be counting money or thinking up your next court case that violates free speech? I heard a cat told a dog to shut up today- sounds like a case."

Jaded rolled her eyes again. "Is free speech so bad, Domino?"

Domino was still concentrating on his magic trick. "Depends on whose free speech you care about. You only seem to care about certain people."

"You're not implying that we at the ACCLU have an agenda, are you?" Jaded said, scandalized.

Domino laughed. "You just keep enjoying the the 1976 Civil Rights Attorney's Fees Awards Act," Domino smiled, realizing he was bothering the lawyer.

"And aren't we entitled to fees awarded to us for the hard work we do in civil rights?"

Domino shrugged. "I think the American people have a hard time believing that the annihilation of the cross from human civilization should be termed a 'civil right.' And yet our tax dollars go into your pockets for just that. You already steal our money- do you want us to thank you too?"

Jaded was visibly upset. "In cities around this beautiful country, people depend on us. San Francisco, Los Angeles, St. Louis, St. Augustine, Corpus Christi, St. Paul, San Jose, San Diego, even the whole state of Maryland."

Domino laughed. "Do you know where any of the names of those places you just mentioned came from?"

Jaded was confused. "No. What do you mean?"

"Nothing."

"Well where do they come from?"

Domino laughed again. "Well I'm not gonna be the one to tell you."

Jaded waved him off. "Just let me see the stupid card-I'll show you the magic trick." She stole a card and did the trick, but Domino wasn't watching. "Domino, look. Look at me. Would you just watch me for a second?"

Domino had had enough. He made a waving gesture with his hand without looking. "Shut up already!"

At the moment of Domino's gesture, however, Gelsomina leaned through the window with Vincent's long cane in her hand. Unnoticed, she clinched Jaded Summers' neck and pounded her against the wall. The inmate fell down limp. Gelsomina disappeared, as Domino looked over, shocked, thinking his magical gesture had done it. He was gazing at his mystic hand when Vincent Fides softly unlocked the front door and slipped past the Chief who was enthralled by the excitement on the television. Vincent freed Domino, and they left without notice.

Outside, Vincent and Anna, Domino and Gelsomina walked victoriously down the street, and away from the jail. Gelsomina told Domino excitedly about the visitation of Mary.

Inside on the television, Federico continued, "I have promised to deliver you, Artcity, some fascinating things about Anthony's past, about who he is, where he came from, and why he is not the lawful owner of the Corporation. I have heard much gossip around Artcity the last few weeks, but the ironic thing is that the curious gossipers have overlooked the one place that holds the secret to Anthony Ceo's identity.

"It is time that all of Artcity know the truth. Anthony Ceo has lied to you. He has told you that there lies within the City a race of ill-bred detractors. He has told you that we, the clowns, are the scourge of Artcity's long and glorious history, that we are the cause of every injustice."

Elsewhere in the world, a frantic Anthony Ceo busted out a window with his elbow.

Federico continued, "He has told you all this even while he performs incredible injustices to Artcity artists, ransacking the artists' creations and selling it to the highest bidders. The artist now has no say, no validity, no power.

"This district that has held Anthony's secret for a decade is, of course, Clown Town. And Anthony's relationship to Clown Town is a little difficult to understand, but, I assure you-"

Chief Petrarch's television suddenly went to snow, the loud, annoying 'Ssssh' sounding like a great, never-ending ocean wave. The Chief was on the edge of his seat, and threw up his hands. He banged on the television repeatedly, trying desperately to retrieve the signal, but to no avail. He finally gave up, muted the television, and plopped back down in his chair exhaustedly.

At the television station studio, Anthony Ceo tried frantically to escape, as he was chased by several security guards. He sprinted through a lawn, hopped a fence, and disappeared into the embracing night.

CHAPTER EIGHTEEN:
THE CONFRONTATION

The midnight bells echoed throughout Artcity, as Vincent escorted Anna to her front door. They kissed softly, and Anna gently opened the door, sneaking in as it was so late. But as the door opened, and the two whispered goodnight, the living room lights burst on, revealing the Mayor, and Congressman Johnson and Anthony Ceo sitting on the couch.

The Mayor rushed forward. "Where the hell have you been?"

Anna was stunned. "Just out, Dad."

Anthony stood up. "With him, huh?" he asked, pointing at the peddler.

The Mayor silenced him: "Anthony." He approached Vincent. "We haven't been properly introduced, kid. I'm the Mayor of Artcity, John Ratio."

Anna said under her breath, "And my father."

"Stop it, Anna," the Mayor scolded. He turned back to Vincent, "You've made quite a name for yourself around here, Vincent, at least among the clowns. I can't say I share in their hospitality."

Anthony approached from the couch. "She's mine, you know. I have her father's signature locked up in a safe."

The Mayor pushed Anthony away. "Sit down, Anthony."

But Anthony persisted. "No! You want to take her from me? You think you can? Are you that powerful, Fides?"

The Mayor pushed Anthony again. "Anthony! Walk away. I don't care who you think you are- that's my daughter. And you don't own a thing but a swindled piece of paper."

Anthony relented, walking into a back room, frustrated.

The Mayor looked back at Vincent. "Now you're gonna leave my daughter alone. And you're gonna go back wherever the hell it is you came from, alone. Got me?"

Vincent stood tall, though. "I'm sorry, sir, but I'm not going anywhere without her." He grabbed Anna's hand.

The Mayor looked to his daughter. "You go to your room- I'll deal with you later."

Anna put her other hand on the clasped hands. "Go to my room? How old do you think I am? I love him, Dad. Don't you want me to have what you had?"

But the Mayor was infuriated. "I presume I said get to your room! For you, Fides, blooming doom is looming from-"

Vincent had an inward revelation. 'They only rhyme when they're really, really mad! That's it!' he thought.

The Mayor continued, "Johnson, take a chair out to the lawn, stay out until dawn- I mean, Stay on- I- Don't take your eyes off that window! I assume you'll have to look out for Prince Valiant here, or his painted friends. I'll call Petrarch to come relieve you in a while."

Congressman Johnson nodded. Vincent looked around the room for some answer to the Mayor. In the back room, he noticed Anthony take off his glasses and rub his eyes, revealing immediately the lightly painted eyes of a clown. Vincent flinched at the sight, looking closer, and realizing Anthony's true identity and secret.

Anna was still looking helplessly to her father. "You're gonna lock me in my room? You can't be serious."

"Sir, you don't understand. I can give her a great life."

But the Mayor wasn't listening. "Get out of my house, kid." The Mayor seized his daughter, pulling her away from Vincent's hand.

Vincent reached out for Anna. "Anna, everything's gonna be fine-"

"Get him out of here!" the Mayor shouted.

Anthony ran in the room, his glasses covering his secret once again, and with Johnson, grabbed the peddler by both arms to escort him out.

Anna threw her father's clamp off of her arm and ran away to her room.

Outside, Congressman Johnson set up his lawn chair, as Anthony walked Vincent to the street. Anthony said slyly, "You can still fight it, Fides. Please don't give up now. I can't wait to prove how worthless you really are."

Vincent stopped him. "I saw your eyes," he said calmly.

"What?!" Anthony cried.

Vincent continued calmly, "I saw them. I know you're a clown. But why would you abandon your people?"

Anthony grabbed his arm again. "If you tell a single soul, I'll make sure Anna never-"

"I won't," Vincent replied patiently.

Shocked by the response, Anthony asked, "What do you mean you won't?"

Vincent explained, "I know how embarrassing it's gonna be for you. And you have to know, it will happen. I know you're scared to death of that day. I'll let you prepare for it."

"Why?" Anthony asked, calming down.

Vincent continued, "Domino is my friend. And he took the blame for your crime. I know you robbed that bank, trying to pin it on me. That's what I'll expose... somehow."

Anthony slyly pitched, "I own that bank- Why the hell would I steal my own money?"

But Vincent shook Anthony's loosened grip off his arm. "It's fine, play dumb. I don't expect you to admit it. Just like I know when this City finds out who you are, it won't be from your lips. You think your lie can last forever."

Anthony grabbed Vincent's arm again, pulling him close. "If you even try to-"

Vincent stopped him. "Excuse me. I may be provoking the most powerful men in this city, but I'm not a criminal. Goodnight, Anthony."

Vincent walked away from the house, patiently strolling down the street, but his mind was less patient, as he desperately sought out the answer to Anna's captor.

Anthony stood there, watching the peddler, wanting to say a thousand things, but unable to shout a word of defense.

In the living room, the Mayor was on the phone. "Frank?" he said into the telephone.

"Yea. Who's this?" the voice responded.

"It's John," the Mayor said with exhaustion in his voice.

The other voice was suddenly nervous. "Oh, uh-How'd you- I mean- How on earth did you find out so fast?"

"Find what out?" the Mayor asked.

Chief Petrarch replied, "Oh. Um- Nothing."

"Frank?" the Mayor lured.

"Yea, sir," the Chief replied nonchalantly.

"Sir?" the Mayor asked, annoyed by unnecessary formality from his friend. "Just say it already."

Chief Petrarch spilled it out. "Domino escaped from jail tonight. It must have been Mary- I told you she constantly gives criminals the keys."

The Mayor was silent on the other end though, taking deep breaths.

"John? John."

The Mayor woke up. "Yea, Frank. Just get over here."

"To your house?" the Chief asked, confused.

"Yea- Get Peire or somebody to find the clown and watch the jail. You'll be staying here for a while."

"Um, doing what, John- can I ask?"

The Mayor paused briefly, then chuckled with disappointment and exhaustion as he realized how stupid his response would sound. "Guarding my daughter," he said finally.

"Oh. Of course."

CHAPTER NINETEEN: REVOLUTION MOMENTUM

Clowns rushed about in Federico's lair, stacking paperwork, typing at computers, hanging blueprints on easels, delivering letters and notes to Federico himself, who stood at a chalkboard before a dozen seated clowns. Federico read a note, smiled confidently, and then wrote in huge letters on the chalkboard, 'M-O-M-E-N-T-U-M.' All the clowns applauded.

Federico silenced them quickly, though. "Brothers and sisters, we move into Artcity in three short days. Begin packing our boxes to move the operation."

While many clowns applauded again, one clown raised his hand. "Sir, I'm still worried about moving our operations next door to the Corporation. Will not Anthony be able to better spy our every intention and move? Clown Town is a fortress that he cannot penetrate."

Federico smiled at the young clown. "How much better for our cause, my young friend. He will be able to watch us intently indeed. But he is already unable to stop us. The Corporation then will see what any condemned man sees at his own public execution: a blade he cannot stop. Remember always to take pity on the man, friends, but the Corporation is a false construct, as lifeless as this chalkboard. Always give love, even to the man who condemns you, but never to a material thing. Anything less than living is not worthy of love, but everything that lives is not only worthy, but entitled to love. So kill the Corporation, but befriend the man.

"This is a new day, brothers and sisters. The tide has turned, and the people have seen the lies they were told. But just because they give you equality is not enough. I do not ask to be 'tolerated,' as they say. I wish to be respected. And that is up to you, clowns. Spread throughout the City, and be good men, good women. Be examples of true virtue. For that is how our tide was turned: they have found that our values are not outdated, not simply old and unusable. They once lost hope in our institution, but it was our love that they wanted back; it was our love they could not live without. Then be sure and always, friends, that you are examples of what they needed from us all along: true, active, selfless, sacrificial, and disinterested love."

The clowns were silent for ten moments as they meditated on the homily, both happy to find progress, and eager to utilize that progress for their true end: building a civilization of life, and love.

As another dark night fell on the Artcity Circle, Vincent slept on a park bench, his fedora tilted over his face. Domino danced around, testing the healing of his once-broken leg. A child rushed up to Domino's delight, joining him in the dance. They danced together, as a concertina's tarantella echoed down from the rooftops.

Suddenly the child's mother approached patiently from a nearby store. Domino slowed a bit, not knowing what to expect. The mother laughed at the sight of her awkward child dancing with glee. She looked at the clown, smiled tenderly, and nodded at him to continue. Domino smiled, too, and danced the child around in circles.

After Domino and the child were satisfied, the mother took her child's hand, motioning him that they needed to get going. Her arm shook with the child's dancing, as she took out a few Clouds and tossed them in a hat beside the dancing clown. She smiled at him, and turned to leave.

Domino stopped her quickly though, and knelt down to pull a small rose out of his hat. He handed it to her with a huge smile. "Thank you."

The mother smiled, too. "You know, for someone as illogical as you are, you're very thoughtful." And she turned again to leave, guiding her child beside her.

Domino was so excited he thought he would burst. He turned to his friend, Vincent, to share his merriment, but realized that he was still sleeping. He was reminded of their problems and sat on a nearby park bench to think.

Vincent was in a hospital room with white walls and radiant white lights overhead. His Anna laid in the hospital bed, clasping his hand, Federico delivering their child. Federico smiled hugely as he finally held the babe, wiping him with towels. He handed the child to the mother, but to Vincent's astonishment, the newborn babe was a black and white spotted dog with a burning torch in his mouth. And Vincent saw suddenly his child rushing across the sky of the earth, the torch sending the radiant white lights of their hospital room to every crevice and corner of the world.

The brilliance of the white light shined so bright that Vincent squinted in his sleep, before finally waking suddenly with an awkward breath. He looked up, and saw Domino seated at the next bench.

Domino looked at Vincent like he belonged in a different room with white walls.

Vincent said to Domino, "Federico."

Domino replied dully, "Okay."

Meanwhile, Anna gazed cautiously out of her tower window. She noticed an empty chair on her lawn and decisively made preparations for her gallant escape. She unraveled the long red carpet, tied one end to her bedpost, and tossed it over her window's ledge- it fell to the ground with the grace of a can of red paint in her morning ritual.

She carefully swung her legs out over the ledge and grabbed the carpet to climb down to her freedom, but just as she readied herself for descent, she heard the front door open. She flew back into her room, whipping the carpet up in after her.

Chief Petrarch didn't notice as he returned to his lawn chair. He sat, crossed his legs, and pulled out his favorite book, Augustine's *Confessions*- he always carried a copy wherever he went. Just before settling in, he glanced up at the tower window, noticed nothing unusual, and so opened his book to a random page to begin reading:

"To whom tell I this? not to Thee, my God; but before Thee to mine own kind, even to that small portion of mankind as may light upon these writings of mine. And to what purpose? that whosoever reads this, may think out of what depths we are to cry unto Thee. For what is nearer to Thine ears than a confessing heart, and a life of faith?"[14]

And thus did the humanist read into the night.

Chapter Twenty:
The Legend of the
Unfaithful

A beautiful morning doesn't ensure a beautiful afternoon, and what starts in the bosom of safety is soon thrown into the fires of danger. Anthony Ceo, Congressman Scotty Johnson, and Chief Frank Petrarch- all born clowns who have lost their paint, and all three epitomizing three entirely different processes.

Ceo's digression was born of free will, that most human power. He knew who he was, but he never allowed his identity to affect how he was meant to act. So when he saw others living under easier paradigms- the criminal, the politician, the businessman- it was rather easy for him to reject his identity for the sake of some individual ambition or desire.

Congressman Johnson's digression was most usual of the three, as millions of clowns lose their paint from his major flaw: ignorance. Johnson never understood what a clown was, or was supposed to be. He didn't understand what it was he rejected. His rejection came more from what others told him the clowns were than what he had ever heard from the clowns themselves. Now, to be honest, this is partly the clowns' fault. Whenever ignorance is at fault, everyone is at fault, for even if Johnson is still culpable in not finding the truth, everyone else is at fault in failing to convey to truth.

Chief Frank Petrarch's loss of identity was wholly different, not born of choice or ignorance but merely perceived by others. The mob sucked the life out of Petrarch, pretending to understand something they couldn't fathom, indeed, using selfish ambitions and desires to distort the old man's identity to their own ends. The human is a social being, built of and for relationship. So although Chief Petrarch loved his identity, and screamed his identity, his identity was stolen from him. Identity theft began with mobs. And Chief Petrarch saw the whole thing happen, too, and was powerless to stop their special interests.

In Clown Town, Vincent Fides, the peddler of dreams, and Domino walked nervously towards an old worn-down home. Vincent had a light sulk in his walk, which Domino was intent on cheering up.

Domino slapped him on the arm. "Come on, Mr. Fides, everything's not so bad. You're too depressed."

Vincent sighed. "Maybe I need some anti-depressants. You got pharmacies around here?"

Domino laughed. "If a pill that's supposed to help with depression has a side effect of suicidal thoughts, I think taking the pill would be a little counter-productive."

Domino changed subjects to hurriedly inform Vincent of various forms of clown etiquette, like signing yourself with the water at the door or bowing at the sound of a certain name. Vincent took it all in, focused on learning the protocol of who he was quickly becoming.

A clown's paint may fall from ignorance, but many people too gain their colors through seeking the truth. It is plain enough that the clowns who walk away are generally ignorant of their very own clownhood, and reject this or that teaching with somebody else's argument. The new-born clowns find their paint often reluctantly, from a mere and humble intention of discovering the truth. In other words, ex-clowns don't understand clownhood, while new clowns are converted precisely by discovering what clownhood means from the outside. And they are indeed welcomed home.

Vincent and Domino approached the door of the old home. Domino knocked. A small rectangular piece of the door slid open, and a big burly clown asked in a big burly voice, "Password?"

Domino said proudly, "ἰχθυς." And the door opened.

The big burly clown asked in his big burly voice, "What's your business here?"

Domino replied, "The peddler to see Federico."

The big burly voice howled back in the house, "The peddler to see Federico!"

Abruptly, a voice came out of a little electronic box on the wall: "Of course. Send him back."

As Vincent and Domino journeyed back in the house, the soft sounds of a piano grew louder and louder. Federico finished the concerto as the boys entered the room, and stood to greet them. "Hey boys." The clown leader walked to his tall leather wingback chair, moving a newspaper out of his way on the desk.

Domino sat.

"We've never really been introduced," Federico said, extending his hand.

"Vincent Fides, the peddler of dreams," Vincent said, shaking the hand firmly.

They both sat. Federico smiled. "You got a dream for me?"

"What can I do?"

Federico folded his hands. "I want freedom."

Vincent laughed. "I can only give so much."

Federico smiled, and then nodded. "Well. You came to see me, right? Maybe I should ask, what can *I* do for you?"

"I'm not sure, exactly. You know my predicament, I take it."

"I do."

Vincent said bluntly, "How can I get my girl?"

"Seems you got the same dream I've got... But why come to me?"

Vincent thought a moment. "Well, we probably have the same dream because we've got the same problems."

Federico said sadly, "Anthony is a lot of people's problem."

Vincent added, "And the Mayor."

But Federico shook his head. "No, John's not. He's still just a father, trying to protect his little girl. You prove to him you're worthy of her hand, you get her."

Vincent was confused. "Then why's Anthony my problem? If I get the Mayor's approval-"

Federico raised his forefinger. "Because Anthony's doing everything he can to make sure the Mayor thinks you're *not* worthy of her."

"Who is he? I know he's a clown."

Federico smiled again. "He's my brother."

Vincent straightened up in his chair.

Federico continued, "Our father was Federico Hart, our mother Josephine Smith."

Vincent said quietly, "Smith?"

"The Smith family has run the Corporation since Artcity's founding. Old man Smith didn't like my father too much. He was a clown, of course, but that didn't matter back then. Far more importantly to the Smiths, he was poor."

Vincent scoffed innocently. "They looked down on him because he was poor?"

Federico continued, "The poor are the scapegoats of history, Mr. Fides. The rich have every resource at hand to create more and more wealth, but the only way they can create more wealth is to gain money from the worker or the consumer, cheaper labor or cheaper products. And for thousands of years, despite modernity's intent to champion itself as the savior of civilization, no one has come up with a functioning system in which there aren't thousands, millions simply left behind.

"The real heroes of our society aren't the politicians and ceos- they're the factory workers who work 70 hours a week just to pay their bills, the custodians, the cooks, the cleaners. These people give their entire lives so the wealthy can run around on trips to Barbados, buy six-digit jewelry, and take their dogs to the spa for canine manicures. It's the poor that run the country, not the rich.

"Oh, I'll admit there are good people who happen to have money- it's not a sin to be rich. But it is simply a fact that the poor struggle and suffer their way through merciless and listless lives in order to give such a convenient lifestyle to the chosen few, and it is that generosity, the generosity of the poor to be poor with dignity, that keeps our society afloat, that gives us hope for the future. The rich folks run around complaining about taxes and stocks and percentage rates, while the poor look for bread.

"Old man Smith thought my father was beneath him, and far beneath his only child. But my father didn't care- he simply refused to go away. He humbly accepted all the criticism and shouts and shoves the old man gave him. But he refused to marry her without her father's consent- it went on for years. And eventually, they won. Old man Smith couldn't believe that my father would just sit there, being yelled at, without offering an ounce of defense. At first, he thought it was weakness, just as he dismissed all poor people- 'He must be a coward,' the old man thought. But with time, the old man saw my father's silence for what it actually was: an incredible strength, an unwavering patience."

Vincent was on the edge of his seat, already formulating his new strategy for winning the Mayor over.

Federico paused for a moment, looking down at his folded hands. Finally, he continued, "Anthony's actually two years older than me, so he couldn't believe it when our parents left the Corporation to me. They didn't trust him. He was simply too selfish for such power. The Smiths sided with Anthony, saying he could pass as a Smith. I look like this- he's only got the eyes, you know. So they destroyed the will, and I got nothing."

Vincent said, "So Anthony started disparaging the clowns to make sure you could never challenge him."

"No," Federico replied calmly. "He didn't reject the clowns for fear of competition. He rejected the clowns because he never tried to live what we teach. Perhaps he was never taught it well enough- we can accept some blame for that. And though he had the very same education I had, he never saw the Beauty of it all. It just never reached him personally. To him, it was customs and traditions and rituals, but there were no deep meanings or purposes behind these physical manifestations of our faith. To him, they were boring.

"To him, to be a clown meant to live a boring and melancholic life without fun and festivals. He never saw that side. He heard teachings he didn't understand, teachings that were and are rather inconvenient for many people to accept. So by taking the truths of the faith superficially, and never really entering into the spirit that animates these truths, they became expendable.

"Ultimately, I suppose, he rejected the clowns for fear of his conscience. It wasn't a superficial decision that those people over there can offer me more than these people here. He had to reject the very fabric of his identity, down to his scarred soul. To acknowledge his clownhood, he would have to acknowledge what he feared most of all: obedience. It's a dirty word these days. To believe that someone else can have authority over you is viewed today as simply old-fashioned naiveté. And he simply wasn't strong enough to be humble, wasn't strong enough to serve others- quite the opposite: he expected everyone else to serve him.

"As for me, he has never been afraid of me challenging him- he cannot believe that I could ever take it away from him. And that is his greatest fault: old hubris. And that will undoubtedly be his downfall, just as it has been his blindfold."

Vincent asked, "What about Marie?"

Federico looked down. "She wanted to stay with the legacy, however she could. She always said that she wanted to stay close to Anthony, so she could eventually expose him, and give the Corporation back to me. But I haven't spoken to her in years. I'm sure that was just a naïve hope... We're close, though- I believe that. The people of Artcity are not idiots. They love this City, and everything it stands for, so if they start hearing the most powerful people saying someone or something is holding the City back, they'll join their voices in opposition. That's the greatest responsibility of the powerful, to keep the people informed. People deserve the truth- they need the truth if they're going to have a chance of understanding what it is they're fighting for."

Vincent smiled. "Like your parents did."

"Like every lover does. Nothing is as strong as love, not the sappy, don't-know-what-to-do-next kind of love, but the fighter. Love can make a warrior out of anybody. That's how I love this City, and the ideal we used to live by. Anthony lost that a long time ago. He was willing to do the one thing an artist can't ever do: lie, just for that little dream come true. Well, even if you get a dream like that, it's not really you that becomes successful. It's a person you created in order to achieve reputation, denying everything you were for that success."

Vincent said confidently, "I know what I want."

Federico smiled. "And I know what I want, Mr. Fides. But all we can do is give everything we have. At the end of the day, even if we can't have what we want so badly, we have to be satisfied with the attempt. Sometimes, dreams don't come true."

Vincent didn't understand. "Sometimes they do."

Federico continued, "If you fight for what you love, and reach with all you've got, at some point, you're going to realize the power and the dignity and the ability that you have- Right there inside you, untapped and unseen. But it is infinitely important that when you find that power, you understand that it was placed there not to serve yourself, but for you to serve others. Maybe what the City needs is more important than my dream. Maybe what the Sage wants out of you and Anna is more important than what you want. There's something going on that is bigger and more important than our whims and desires. You have to do the very best with what you've been given."

"What is it? What's more important than my love?"

"Do you know what Providence is, Mr. Fides?" Federico asked.

"Something like economy, right?"

Federico smiled and nodded. "Something like that, sure. You've got a purpose to serve here, Mr. Fides. You've got a place here in Artcity, too. And until you can figure out what you've got to give us, you're going to be frustrated at every turn. You can't peddle here because we clowns and artists alike are going to ask more from you than a shiny trinket or a dancing toy. We need you to be something more than you've ever seen in yourself before."

"What?" Vincent asked. "What can I give?"

"I can't answer that for you, Mr. Fides. It's not my purpose."

Vincent asked quickly, "Then how can I find out? The Sage? The concertina guy? Who can help me?"

Federico looked right into Vincent's eyes. "What if there's no one who can help you? What if something depends solely and unavoidably on you?"

Vincent looked down at the ground, obviously uncomfortable as much by the question as by Federico's piercing gaze. Vincent said, "Anthony never found that purpose for himself. That's why he ran from his family. That's why he says so many bad things about you. Because he sees your purpose but not his?"

"Sure. Without purpose, we cannot join Providence, so in jealousy and frustration, we seek to destroy it."

Vincent looked up, and right into Federico's eyes. "Then all I can do is become the best possible Vincent Fides that I can become, and be him for others."

Federico smiled. "There are many, many people in this world, even clowns, who waste all their time chasing mirages, apparitions of happiness or safety or security, whatever they think will be good lives. But when they chase those mirages, there is an unavoidable moment lurking: when the illusion disappears.

"They spend their whole lives in idle recreations and games, reading books and watching films of appalling values and messages about what this life is really about. They even bring old, tired arguments from outsiders to use against their own family, and simply because they get their ideas from their own enemies. They get their views of life and love and happiness from a culture that tells them to chase money, sex, and possessions, all the possessions you can possibly stuff in your house. And then, just maybe then, when you don't have enough space in your house to walk around because of the piles and piles of junk- maybe then, you'll be happy.

"You are what you eat, Mr. Fides. The old adage holds well today in the third millennium. If you eat lust, you will lust. If you fill your mind with all sorts of lustful images that turn our opposite sexes into mere objects for our own pleasure, mere toys that please us when we're in the mood, you will in turn treat them that way. And a woman will become to you as interesting and as trivial as a deck of cards or a remote control. You will become what you eat."

Vincent said, "So I can spend my time listening to Jaded Summers or the Sage, and allow the one I choose to change me."

Federico smiled. "I heard a beautiful story once. At any given moment, within every single human being on earth, there are two different lions fighting to the death. Each lion wants complete control of the man. This intense war has been violently enduring for as long as the man can remember. But the battle is to the death, so one of these lions will indeed someday win. Now some people are terrified of the day that war ends: they anxiously wonder which one it will be- who will win? But the champion is not so hard to decipher. It is easy to tell who the victor will be: it will be the lion that the man feeds. So a man may feed himself with lust and greed and selfishness and lies, and then watch himself be devoured by his passions. Or a man may feed himself with patience and generosity and humility and truth, and then watch himself be devoured by a better self. One of these lions must win. But which one will it be?"

Chapter Twenty-One: Love that Saves

The stars were aligning that night, but Anna wasn't an astronomer. In the tower prison, Bambina brushed Anna's hair, a rather futile effort since Anna's hair barely reached her shoulders, but tradition is tradition.

Anna asked, "Am I asking for too much?"

Bambina scolded her. "You can't think like that."

Anna said exhaustedly, "I don't know what to think anymore."

Bambina continued brushing as a question plagued her mind. She finally could not conceal it any longer. "Do you love him? I mean, really love him, need him- can't deal without him- all that stuff?"

Anna wasn't offended by the question, but replied plainly, "How am I doing?"

Bambina laughed. "He'll come for you."

"The old rescue fairytale?"

Bambina rolled her eyes. "I wish it was just a fairytale. Life is a lot harder."

Anna sat silently.

Bambina finally said, "He'll come, though. We know that much."

After a moment, there was a knock at the bedroom door. Both were expectant for a moment, but quickly realized how improbable it would be for Vincent to be here already.

Anna said loudly, and unsurely, "Yes?"

Anthony Ceo entered the room, frightening Anna.

"Anthony!" Anna exclaimed, as she ran to her robe to cover herself.

Anthony approached. "I'm sorry, Anna. I just needed to see you. Will you excuse us, Bambina?"

Bambina replied quickly, "I don't think that's such a good idea."

But Anna said, "It's okay, Bambina."

"Are you sure?" Bambina asked in amazement.

"I'll be fine."

Bambina left the room and closed the door, but listened as closely as she could.

Anna sat on her bed. "You could have chosen a better time. I could have been sleeping by now."

"Your father told me you haven't been sleeping lately."

Anna was surprised to hear that her father would tell Anthony anything. "What else has he told you?"

Anthony took a deep breath. "Among other things, that you don't want to marry me."

Anna got up from the bed, and walked swiftly to the window. With her back to Anthony, she said, "I suppose you're going to tell me how much you love me and expect me to run into your arms."

But Anthony chuckled. "No- No... Hell, I don't even know what love is, Anna." Anthony sat down on the bed. After a moment, Anthony said, "Do you know?"

Anna's heavy head lowered. "Not anymore. Not after this."

"I could never make you happy, could I."

Anna paused. "No."

Anthony gathered himself and stood up to face her. "The peddler?"

Anna smiled gently. "Maybe."

Anthony tried to understand. He asked sharply, "Why him?"

Anna lifted her head and faced him. "I don't know really. I may be here, locked in this tower prison, but I could leave if I really wanted to, and my Dad knows that. I'm not a helpless girl being held down by the men who love me. I choose to be here, because it doesn't make sense to my Dad for me to be where I want to be. So I'll give him time. I'll give Vincent time. I love them both, and that's why I'm here: locked in my room, but staring out the window.

"I've thought about leaving. Is it more powerful for me to run away, or more powerful to stay and fight for what I want? I don't know anymore. It just doesn't seem worth it sometimes. But I know I love him- I have to. He's the one I'm thinking about. He's why I can't take my eyes off that window, not so he can come and save me, but so I can leave this prison, and save him."

Anthony's head grew heavy now. He looked down at Anna's feet, not wanting to look in her eyes. He thought a moment for something else, anything else to say. But he found nothing. He finally said, almost whispered, "I'm sorry for coming so late." He turned and walked sharply out of the room, closing the door behind him.

Anna journeyed back to her window and watched Anthony walk past Chief Petrarch in the lawn.

Chapter Twenty-Two: Sight for the Blind

For the first time since Vincent Fides, the peddler of dreams, arrived in Artcity, he thought about leaving. He understood that he could only be himself, and be himself for others, but maybe what the Sage wanted out of him was more important than what he wanted. Maybe Anna would indeed be better off without him. He appreciated Federico's story about the passionate patience it took to win over a disapproving father, but Vincent wondered if he had such patience. He forgot how to peddle so long ago, he barely remembered his standard pitches, and his confidence left with his abilities. What did he have to offer such a city, such a people, such a woman?

Federico had suggested Vincent come back to the Sage once more before he considered leaving, so Vincent, respecting Federico, obliged. As Vincent and Domino approached Rustici Palace, though, Vincent was so dejected, he didn't even know what to say. He felt half the man he used to be. He was once so sure of himself, so confident. Today, after the wars of Artcity politics and economy, a whole vibrant culture opposing his happiness, he was a shell of a man, humble and meek, unsure and weary.

The clown guide led the foreigner into Rustici Palace. As the two passed Jaded Summers, ACCLU, they didn't even look in her direction, for though they didn't know the direction to take, the path that would lead them to their happy ending, they knew that direction wasn't with her. Jaded had become a shell of a woman to them, a computerized voice with old, stale arguments and word-choices that embarrass the dictionary. She couldn't think for herself. Vincent couldn't live for himself.

Jaded smiled as they passed her, still confident in her superficial world. "They're all just holding you back, Mr. Fides," she said in a somber tone.

Domino held back at a distance, as Vincent Fides approached the vacant chair of the Sage.

The Sage beamed with a glowing smile, "Doin' better taday, Mista Fides?"

Vincent sat. "I'm a little confused, Sage."

The Sage chuckled. "Well, i's normal. Jus' stick to water 'n soup fer a day, you'll shake it off."

Vincent forced a smile. "I was hoping for a few words instead."

The Sage broke out his shining gear and went to work. "You were hopin' I could tell ya what ta do, how ta get her. I can't, Mista Fides. You guys gotta lern ya gotta lot more power than ya think. You come ta me, 'stead a goin' ta her."

"I care about her," Vincent said honestly.

The Sage didn't look up from the shoes. "Me, too. So what?"

Vincent tried again. "I want what's best for her."

The Sage looked up, but repeated, "Me, too. So what?" He paused a moment as he went back to work. "You startin' ta doubt that *you're* what's best fer her?"

"Her father doesn't think so. Maybe I'm not," Vincent said wearily.

The Sage kept at his rags, not acknowledging Vincent's deduction.

Vincent sighed. "I just feel like the whole weight of the world's on my shoulders."

The Sage laughed, "Well, it's probly those shoulder pads in that ugly suit. Look- Our tale's about Providence, Mista Fides, 'at's all. Now sure air's a lotta people tryna mess up that Providence, tryna put up all kinds a stumblinblocks fer good people, but at tha end a tha day, ya can't stop a good man from bein' good. He gonna be himself.

"Take me fer instance. Miz Summers ova there tries with everything she's got to keep people away from me. Why? Cuz she knows plain well what I'm here ta tell 'em. I exist for two reasons, Mista Fides, 'n two reasons only: one, ta tell all you folk what ya already know deep down inside, but can't hear too clearly cuz a all the noise Miz Summers 'n her kin spit out. 'N two, ta clean ya up, 'n make you shine. That's it, Mista Fides. No glorious fame and applause and money and all that nonsense ya'll run around chasin'. Just to be a voice you can recognize, and clean ya up. It's a humble little existence when ya think about it, but i's mine- i's what I was put here ta do. You was put here fer somethin' too, ya gotta believe it. Now I can't read the stars 'n tell ya if you gonna get that girl or not- I don't know if you're s'posed ta get that girl. But I can tell ya this, and this is all I got: ya gotta be you.

"Ferget pawnin' all those little figurines for a little while- at's why it was taken away from ya. Bein' a peddler's just what ya do, it ain't who ya are. Ya never knew that person before, and at's why havin' your abilities stoled from ya has hurt so bad. But until you find out what ya got to offer that beautiful Providence, then you're not even here- you ain't even been born yet."

Vincent took a deep breath. "I'm trying, Sage. I'm trying as hard as I know how."

The Sage was already cleaning again. "I know ya are, Mista Fides, 'n i's okay ta get hurt and weary every once in a while. But yer opportunities are comin' up quick, 'n you better be ready when they come."

Vincent sat up a little in his seat. "Opportunities?"

The Sage smacked Vincent's shoes with his rags. "Opportunities are inevitable. You go hide yer head in the desert fer forty years, ya still gonna get some incredible opportunities. The whole point a life is to get ready, every moment, every day- get ready fer when they come."

"An opportunity to get Anna?"

The Sage chuckled a bit while he worked. "The clowns has finally made their opportunity for theyselves. Nobody'd listen to 'em fer years now, but they never gave up. They kept truckin' along, bein' theyselves and hopin' fer an opportunity to show them beautiful selves to the world. 'At's all you can do, too, Mista Fides. Keep marchin' along til that opportunity comes."

Vincent didn't know what to say. He was actually thinking about marching out of Artcity when the Sage looked up at the sky. Vincent followed his upward gaze but didn't know what he was looking at.

The Sage looked at the sky with the same care and precision that he always aimed at shoes ready to be cleaned. Finally, without looking down, he said, "I's a lil' cloudy taday. I bet i's gon' rain come tha mornin'. You seen it rain yet since ya been here?"

Vincent was confused. "I- I guess not... Rain's rain, right?"

The Sage smiled. "Nope. Rain's paint here in Artcity. None a that clear, liquid stuff- just colored, flammable gunk. Stuff ya can build somethin' with, know what I mean?"

Vincent was still confused. "No."

"Don't rain too often, though," the Sage went on. He made a large circular gesture with one hand, and said, "Whole circulation thing's different... I tell you what, you come here lookin' fer answers, huh?"

Vincent said dully, "Yea."

The Sage never stopped. "Well, I ain't got 'em. But when it rains paint, hm, then you'll see clearer thin ya e'er did before- 'At I kin promise ya. You just havta remember one important thing, Mista Fides: Nothin's gonna change 'til you do." Vincent didn't really have a response, so the Sage looked over to Domino. "Hey, Domino! Come on over here, boy!"

Domino was startled, jumping tremendously at the sound of his name from the Sage's mouth. He nervously joined the other two.

The Sage turned back to Vincent. "You don't mind, do ya Mista Fides? He's never had a shine."

Vincent nodded as he stood up from the seat. Domino replaced him in the chair, slowly, nervously, yet proudly.

The Sage looked down and laughed. "Look at dem shoes! This could take a while, Mista Fides."

Domino was still stunned. "It's nice to meet you... the Sage of Rustici Palace."

The Sage bent down and went to work. "'Sage' is fine, Domino. I hear you wanna open a theatre- At's excitin'... Seems like you deserve some kinda reward fer all yer sacrificin' round here."

Vincent stared up at the sky, trying to figure out what on earth the Sage had just told him. High above Rustici Palace, a scared father watched him. And just beyond the fence line, Marie Smith watched, too. It seemed all of Artcity was watching Vincent stare up at the sky that day, wondering about the future of their lives that he held in his gaze.

Chapter Twenty-Three: The Art of Sacrifice

Unfortunately for the human being, just as opportunities are sure to come and sure to go, suffering is sure to come and sure to go. The problem of evil is not so difficult as Anthony's philosophers make it out to be, for though God surely exists and is all-good and all-powerful, so does man exist, and is not all-good nor all-powerful. And all our bitter, little complaints and greedy, little actions bring consequences that echo throughout a community, a society, a planet, and beyond.

And yet humanity has been blessed by a Lord that is so inebriated by love and goodness that He can do nothing but take every solitary thing, animate and inanimate alike, and give it meaning, purpose, and direction. All things in existence bend towards Him, the central gravitational pull of the universe, not located in time nor space, with galaxies revolving around Him like a big old black hole, but located in all time and all space, with all the material universe shooting like comets right to His glowing face. He can find a way to bring goodness and wisdom even from our most atrocious massacres and tragedies, which is why even the most militant of atheists can still be the most impressive of philanthropists. And despite all the acidic rampages against some system of dogmatic theology they don't even understand, they indeed have love and goodness, stamped as they are with the image of God, and bend towards Him as the reluctant surf rushes towards the coast.

Humanity is good. Deep down at our core, covered though it may be by piles of trash and collected junk like antique furniture or ceramic dolls, the human person is a beautiful, powerful, good thing. We can only hide our goodness, ignore our goodness, even despise our goodness- but we cannot kill it. It will always tug on our sleeves like our children do, asking for a little attention.

We understand though that goodness comes with a price. One Yes includes a million No's. But no matter the price, goodness is well worth the sacrifice.

Chief Petrarch sat guarding the princess in the tower, the trouble-making daughter of a good friend. It may be a stiff price, but friendship too demands sacrifice. He sat reading and editing his own meditations on the many distractions and obstacles humanity has placed in their own way.

Agendas are as old as tribes, and paradigms as many as the stars in the sky. What must matter is something that is shared, something that unifies all creation, not separates. Old Veritas. Truth. There is such a thing- the word was not invented to describe an abstract idea, but instead, a concrete, real, living answer. Whether the stars being exploded into existence and all the material universe with them was a mere chance, a mere coincidence, a mere chaotic moment in the history of universal time, or whether a first being willed all things into existence out of love and for the purpose of a loving relationship with Him, there is indeed an answer. Truth exists. Backed up from a safe distance, in order to see a larger picture of life on earth, to rage on in those little political parties, or lobbies, or profit-seekers, or news-peddlers is a rather futile and ridiculous existence. Like opportunities or suffering, life will come and life will go. A person will be remembered for a brief time perhaps, but will be forgotten, and subsequent generations will invent their own personalities to apply to the dead name, in order to add substance and authority to their own limited and ignorant agendas.

Oh, life lived in separation, where is thy attraction? But the Sage as usual was right- no one can stop the good from being good. And so while the Corporation or the Media may rage on in their limited and ignorant agendas, they may also bend towards Truth. They may also rise above the mortality of their fickle fashions and momentary ideas to seek what has mattered all along: Veritas. Humanity will die without it- consumed by our own ambitions. If all nations want the same throne, only one shall succeed, and they only briefly before the next revolution. Oh, life lived in greedy ambition, where is thy joy? To rule is only to be alone, nothing more. The only true leader will make himself last, for to lead is active and therefore is to serve.

Anna watched Chief Petrarch from her window, wondering what he was writing about. She had all but given up on Old Veritas, simply because He hadn't given her what she wanted. She knew Vincent would come, and she would run as fast as she could, as far away from everything she had ever known, the City, the suitor, the kind people, and even her father. This life wouldn't bend towards her, so she would run.

Lost in meditation, Anna didn't notice Vincent Fides, the peddler of dreams, Domino, and Gelsomina sneakily approach to hide in the bushes of her side yard. Chief Petrarch's eyes were on the book in his hands, so he didn't notice either.

The three huddled in the bushes, arms around each other like a grade-school football team. Vincent whispered something, and they all nodded in agreement.

Gelsomina turned away from the huddle and took a deep breath, knowing her job in the mission would be a tough one. But whatever the price, serving a higher cause always includes sacrifice. She left the cover of the bushes and walked along the sidewalk right up to Chief Petrarch. Gelsomina called, "Heya, Chief!"

Chief Petrarch, startled from shifting his eyes from his own mortality to a young approaching clown, called back, "Hey, Gelsomina. What're you doing walking around here this time of night?"

Gelsomina was prepared. "Deputy Peire sent me, said you needed a break." We'll leave the lying lecture for another time.

Chief Petrarch laughed. "After what happened at the theatre, I'd be crazy to let you stand guard for me. I mean, no offense, Gelsomina, but no thanks."

Gelsomina pulled a huge, oversized pocket-watch out of her little pocket, waving it violently and uncomfortably in Petrarch's face. She lowered her voice as deeply as she could. "I know you're tired, Chief. Tired."

Chief Petrarch chuckled a little. "What are you doing, Gelsomina?"

Gelsomina cried louder and deeply, "Tired! Tired!"

The Chief closed his book, amused at the clown's show. "Are you actually trying to hypnotize me?"

But Gelsomina yawned loudly as she lied down slowly, curling up into a little ball. Her cadence grew faint with her energy. "Tired... Tired." After a brief moment of silence as the Chief watched on, Gelsomina began snoring loudly.

On the third snore, Chief Petrarch softly tapped her arm. He whispered, "Gelsomina." He tapped her a little harder. He spoke a little louder, "Gelsomina!"

Gelsomina woke suddenly, "What? Who?"

Chief Petrarch just shook his head. "I am tired, Gelsomina, but, thanks anyways."

Vincent and Domino were watching from the bushes. They looked at each other, aware that their plan was not going quite as planned.

Gelsomina sat up, yawning. "Um, the theatre? Yea, you see, at the theatre, I was just- Ooo- I was just tired myself. And that's what happens when you- when you're tired."

Chief Petrarch gently placed his book beside himself on the ground. "I'll tell you what, Gelsomina. How about you just stick around and keep me company for a while?"

After several different emotions crossed her face, Gelsomina hesitatingly agreed, "Alright." Neither knew quite how to begin a conversation, though, so after a moment, they both yawned together.

In the bushes, Vincent and Domino shook their heads. They huddled back together to try to find a new and better idea. Domino found the first idea and pulled away from the huddle, but it was obvious to Vincent that Domino didn't like his idea. Finally, Domino sighed, deciding what he must do. Domino knew the price, but his courage would never let him fear sacrifice.

Vincent whispered, "What?"

Without answering, Domino walked out from behind the bushes and onto the street. Gelsomina realized what Domino's plan was before Vincent did, and she stood, pointed, and howled, "Criminal!"

Petrarch looked up, startled again. When he saw Domino, he leapt from his seat to go catch him. Gelsomina waddled swiftly behind him, as they chased Domino down the street.

Vincent seized the opportunity granted him, and dashed for the window. They caught Domino quickly, though. As Vincent began to climb the trellis, he immediately snapped a twig loudly with his first clumsy step. Petrarch reacted to the twig, but just before his eyes journeyed back to the window, Marie Smith swept Vincent up and escaped to the hidden side-yard. Domino and Gelsomina immediately distracted the Chief to dissuade him from investigating.

Anna reacted to the commotion too, coming back over to her window. She watched as Chief Petrarch slapped handcuffs on Domino in her front yard. She called to him, "Domino!"

Domino looked up with embarrassment in yet another sacrifice for her sake. He nodded at her, "Princess."

Anna of course immediately thought of Vincent, who must have been close by. She looked everywhere in the yard, behind the bushes, down the street, but she found him nowhere.

Out front, Gelsomina had another idea. "Ooo- Ooo. I'll take him to the station, Chief."

Chief Petrarch replied, "No.- No! *I'll* take him. He's not getting away from me again. Gelsomina, I'll be back in ten minutes. Please. Don't take your eyes off that window."

Domino winked at Gelsomina as he was led away, the best applause he could manage for her great performance. Gelsomina beamed back at him, proud of herself. She watched admiringly as Domino was led down the street.

On the side of the house, Vincent was brushing dirt off his pants. Smith and Vincent tried to catch their breaths.

Smith said exhaustedly, "You're so clumsy."

Vincent responded, "Thank you."

Smith nodded. "I don't know how much you know, so I'm afraid I don't know where to begin."

Vincent assured her, "I know everything."

Smith chuckled. "That I doubt. But I assume that means you know about my family, all of them."

Vincent nodded. "And the bank robbery."

Smith looked down at the ground. "Are you going to expose Anthony as a clown?"

Vincent shook his head. "That wouldn't get the Corporation back in Federico's hands." Smith looked up as she heard Federico's name. Vincent continued, "He holds nothing against you. He understands why you stayed."

Smith shook the emotions off. "It does not matter. What are you going to do?"

But Vincent replied quickly, "What are you gonna do? That's my question."

Smith was confused. "I do not know how- I have been trying for years."

Vincent shrugged. "The bank robbery."

Smith looked down again. "Take the blame for Anthony? I could not-"

Vincent asked, "Even if it means the Corporation returns to what it was? That Artcity returns to what it was?"

Smith looked up. "It broke my heart, too. Every moment with Anthony, I kept telling myself that someday- I could…"

Vincent interrupted her, "You could confess the bank robbery."

"And go to jail?"

"And take Anthony with you. If he goes to jail, then-"

"Jail?" Smith asked softly.

After a brief silence, Vincent smiled gently, and joked, "I might be able to get the Mayor's pardon someday… Maybe."

Smith allowed a small smile briefly, but quickly returned to her decision. She looked up at him, "The peddler of dreams, huh?"

Vincent smiled. "Just a chance to make things right."

Smith nodded. "Go see your girl."

Vincent looked back towards the front, then back at Smith. "You'll be here when I get back?"

Smith smiled. "Of course I will… Jail's a small price to pay for a dream come true." Smith finally submitted to an idea that had plagued her conscience for years: No one likes the price, but even justice demands sacrifice.

Vincent tipped his hat to Smith, then dashed to the front, and up the trellis, calling Anna's name as he neared the top.

Congressman Johnson watched Smith from a window on the side of the house, listening intently with an expensive pen and a notebook in his hands.

Anna rushed to Vincent, meeting him with a strong kiss. But Anna quickly left Vincent to climb by himself as she slapped a huge suitcase on her bed, throwing clothes into it frantically. Vincent climbed up onto the ledge and entered the room.

Vincent said calmly, "What are you doing?"

Anna didn't stop, or even look at him. "I'm packing. We've got to get out of here...-" She stopped a moment and looked at him, "That's- That's why you came, right?"

After a pause, Vincent muttered, "Yes- Yea, of course."

Anna continued packing. "We just need to get as far away from this place as possible, where my Dad and Anthony and corporations and contracts can't harm us. Nothing unique happens here- Artcity is just like any other city. It's all money and power and-"

But Vincent interrupted her in a daze, "It rains paint here."

Anna stopped, confused. "It what?"

Vincent said confidently, "It rains paint."

Anna laughed. "Who told you that?"

"The Sage."

Anna continued packing, flying all over her room to gather things. "Well, I don't know what he was talking about- It rains water here, like everywhere else-"

"We can't," Vincent said quietly.

"We can't what?" Anna asked, not stopping.

Vincent walked over and held her hand away from the suitcase. "Stop- Anna, stop it... We can't leave."

Anna didn't understand. "Why not?"

Vincent sat down, guiding her down with him. "I don't know how to explain it all. Whatever it is that's going to happen, I know it's here. We can't run away."

Anna shot back, "Is this because of the Sage? The Sage can only tell you so much- you can't trust him with your life, Vincent-"

"It's- It's not him," Vincent began. "Anna, listen. I love you- you know I do. And that's why we have to do this right. I want your father's approval. I don't want to steal you away from him. If your father doesn't accept us now, then he'll just have to get used to *me* camping in your front lawn. I'm not giving up."

The peddler of dreams finally learned the secret of life: You could never imagine the price, but love is sacrifice.

Anna didn't know what to say. "Just tear my heart out and throw it like a baseball."

Vincent made a nasty face. "Is that a medieval joke?"

Anna said in a daze, "We may never have this chance again, Vincent."

Vincent stood up. "Trust me, Anna. Just trust me. I'll be back soon."

Anna nodded. "I love you- I'll do anything you tell me."

Vincent smiled. "You sound like a lobbyist."

Anna laughed as Vincent rushed to the window and began climbing down. She believed in him. She was afraid of what might happen in the days ahead. But though fear was the price, she knew hope includes sacrifice.

Anna rushed to the window. "Wait- Wait!"
Vincent looked up at her.

Anna said, "It rains water." Vincent climbed back up and kissed her, then dashed down the trellis. Gelsomina and Smith joined him on the lawn, pulling his gaze away from Anna, and Anna watched as the three figures disappeared into the night.

CHAPTER TWENTY-FOUR: FREEDOM

The deep dark night was dimly lit by seven spacious flashlights. Vincent Fides, the redeemed peddler of dreams, Gelsomina, Marie Smith, her brother Federico, and three clowns marched on the jail with patient while forceful steps. Mary stood atop the jail, smiling at the coming procession.

Vincent reached the door first and opened it for his assembly to enter. Domino stood up in his cell. Deputy d'Alvernhe sat up in his chair at the desk. Chief Petrarch, standing beside him, looked up from his paperwork. The Chief saw Gelsomina enter first. "Gelsomina?! Why aren't you staring at a certain window?!"

Gelsomina calmed him. "But Vincent's right here, Chief. He can't be at Anna's if he's right here."

Vincent approached the Chief. "Hey there, Chief Petrarch."

The Chief nodded. "Peddler. Can I help you?"

Vincent presented Smith. "Marie Smith here robbed the bank last week, at the order of her boss, Anthony Ceo. Domino is innocent."

Petrarch was not surprised. He looked to Smith. "That true, Miss Smith?"

Smith stepped forward. "Yes. It's not the first time we've used crime to achieve our objectives. But I can't go on like this." She looked at Federico, and paused. Then, looking back to the Chief, she said, "We... are criminals."

Petrarch asked, "Will he resist arrest?"

Smith thought a moment. "I don't- I'm not sure anymore. He's been acting so strangely lately."

The Chief looked over at Domino with a small smile, and began fumbling through his keys to release him.

Suddenly, Deputy Bernart de Ventadorn entered the jail, leading a handcuffed Anthony Ceo behind him.

The Chief dropped his keys. "Bernart! How'd you know?"

Anthony spoke up bitterly, "What is this? What are they all doing here?"

The Chief walked over to greet Anthony. "Shut up, Anthony. You're under arrest for conspiracy to commit bank robbery."

Deputy de Ventadorn was confused, though. "Uh, Chief? He's under arrest for breaking and entering at the ACTV Network Headquarters... and loitering in the parking lot before and after."

Petrarch smiled. "What?"

The deputy continued, "Yea. Mother sent us the surveillance tapes this morning. He broke in to pull the plug on Federico's speech."

Anthony looked down at the ground. With disgust, he said under his breath, "The Media."

Petrarch leaned in on Anthony. "Anthony? Anything you'd like to add?"

But Smith spoke up quickly. "He was talking about it all week. He wanted me to do it, but I told him I couldn't do this anymore."

Anthony stopped her, though. "I can speak for myself, Marie. Yes, Chief, it's true." He paused a moment to take a deep breath. "I've done a lot I'm not proud of over the past few years. Business is business. But I'll pay the consequences of the City." He looked suddenly to Federico. "Power's the greatest temptation there is."

Chief Petrarch unlocked and opened Domino's cell door, and Domino joined his crowd between Vincent and Gelsomina. Smith walked voluntarily into the cell. After a moment of Petrarch waiting for Anthony to walk in, the clowns took him by the arms and escorted him to the cell. Petrarch began to close the cell door, but was interrupted by Federico who stepped forward.

"Wait, Chief," Federico said as he approached the cell. "Power can be used with great virtue, too, brother. But it demands honesty." He removed Anthony's glasses. "You won't need these anymore."

Petrarch and the deputies were shocked as they noticed Anthony's clown eyes. Federico guided the frozen Petrarch out of the way as he closed the cell door in front of Anthony.

Anthony said quietly, "Alright, Federico."

Domino tugged on Vincent's arm. "Thank you, Mr. Fides."

But Gelsomina tugged Domino's arm. "Ooo- Ooo- What about me?"

Domino looked over to her and smiled. "Yes of course. Thank you, too… darling." He kissed her on the cheek.

Gelsomina blushed. "Ooo… darling."

Smith called from the cell though to interrupt them. "Guys! Go earn my pardon, please."

Vincent looked to the door with a smile, and rushed out. Everyone except the deputies joined him at a more patient pace.

CHAPTER TWENTY-FIVE: STILL PEDDLIN

The heresy- Excuse me- The fallacy of this particular dark age of human civilization was the myth that to believe anything, to live your life according to any systematic, sustainable set of convictions was too confrontational to produce human prosperity. And so we believed in nothing, and lived that nothingness. The world was governed by nihilism instead of true secularism, anarchy instead of order, apathy instead of knowledge. Any growth of such a culture would soon reveal its own futility though. And so we watched this nihilism consume us. And because we refused to acknowledge any real differences among us, we were powerless to deal with those differences. And with a lack of any human reason or common sense, the culture fell into a passionate and immature emotionalism.

The world at the beginning of the 21st century was one of the most powerful forms of tribalism, but nothing more, nothing impressive or gallant or heroic, no golden age. We were an epoch of irrational animals, denouncing everything in the beautiful human spirit that could have given us rise above the animal kingdom. 'Survival of the fittest' was our battle cry, money and possessions our life force. Perhaps the worst problem was that the bad people didn't know they were bad, or didn't even believe in badness. So they defended deception and wordplay as truth, murder as privacy, lawlessness as progress, dehumanization as profit, politics as policy, smut as art, and lust as love.

Yet amidst this powerful culture of death, powerful voices rose to confront the masses, to face the persecution and criticism that is always due the true bringers of progress, peace, and Providence. They walked calmly before the firing squad to allow their own beliefs to stand the test of the culture's bullets. And no matter what ridicule or belittling they were sure to face, they could not stand down- they could not be happy in a cave or a desert, for it was their vocation to engage the world on the world's own terms. They sought Truth, and wouldn't settle for less. They sought Love, and shined with the loot of their every day's adventure.

There have never been words uttered in the whole history of the world that so confound the human mind, that so challenge the human spirit, than these: "Love your enemy." This shocking statement seems absolutely contrary to everything the human mind can comprehend. 'Why would I love my enemy? I will hurt my enemy, destroy my enemy.' But the chosen few are called to live these most revolutionary words, and live them they do. It is out of love that the voices spoke up, out of love that the seekers of Truth screamed out against the lies and deception of an Age of Unreason, a delightened era of pomposity the likes of which would make old Rome and her Caesars blush.

And it is out of love that these brave men and women, heroes of humanity, faced their own deaths not with tears and fears, but with joyful songs. They welcomed Brother Death in their own homes, locked into a destiny that they could not run away from. For though they could live elsewhere in relative security, they would sacrifice the very same death, for dead would be the man's honor, his dignity, his glory. And he would run off to live someone else's life. No- the brave ones stay and fight, and losing their lives, gain them.

The Mayor watched from his window as Vincent Fides, the brave peddler of dreams, Domino, Gelsomina, Federico, Chief Petrarch, and several clowns marched down the street to his own house. Anna, locked in her tower prison, heard the approaching commotion, and came to her window to watch as well. Her eyes lit up when they met her Vincent.

As the entourage entered the lawn, the Mayor opened his front door to meet them, holding a glass of wine in his hand. His face was solemn, cold, not from disdain or hatred, but from an exhaustion of fighting forces that were more powerful than him, and a looming submission he saw plainly before his eyes. The world as he knew it was ending, and he knew it. He did not care about clowns or corporations, mind you- he cared for only two things in the world: the City it was his job to govern, and the daughter it was his life's work to protect. Both of his great loves were changing, not out of disdain or hatred, but out of new loves and opportunities.

The assembly stopped in the front lawn. The Mayor pointed at Petrarch with his wine glass. "You." Then at Federico. "You." And then at Vincent. "And you." And the Mayor returned into his house. The three delegates followed after him, Anna watching every step.

In the living room, the Mayor sat and crossed his legs. The three stood in a line in front of him. The Mayor looked to Petrarch. "Why's the cavalry on my lawn?"

Chief Petrarch said, "Anthony's been arrested, John."

The Mayor was not surprised, but replied plainly, "For what?"

The Chief began, "Conspiracy to commit bank robbery, and breaking and entering at ACTV, and loitering. It's been hinted that there have been other crimes as well. I just don't know how cooperative he'll be."

The Mayor looked at Federico. "I knew your father pretty well. He was a good man. I was surprised to hear he gave the Corporation to Anthony in the first place."

Federico smiled gently. "He didn't, sir."

The Mayor realized Federico's meaning quickly enough, and again was not surprised. The Mayor finally matched Federico's small smile. "You up for the job?"

Federico straightened. "Yes, sir. Ready to restore my family and my City to what I remember as a child."

After a pause, the Mayor looked at Vincent- he sighed and rolled his eyes. "And what are you doing here, peddler? Trying to mooch off the clowns' happy ending?"

Vincent smiled, and not gently. "I'm here to ask you for your daughter's hand, sir."

The Mayor replied, "You should've taken her when you had the chance."

Vincent's brow creased. "How did you-?"

"I'm the Mayor, son- I've got more security than cops and clowns."

Vincent lifted his chin slightly. "I didn't want to run, because I think we each have something the other wants, something we can do for each other."

The Mayor finally smiled. "Still peddlin', huh? I'm not good at, uh- Thank you for not taking her away from me. You got a future in mind for yourself?"

Vincent didn't quite understand, though. "Other than your daughter, sir?"

The Mayor said quickly, "Yes, peddler, other than my daughter."

Vincent looked over to the clown beside him. "I'm sure Federico could find something important for a salesman to do."

Both Vincent and the Mayor eyed Federico. When Federico finally realized they were waiting on a response, he nodded quickly.

The Mayor looked down at the ground and bit his lip. "I'm not gonna get rid of you, am I."

Vincent smiled again. "No, sir."

The Mayor nodded to himself. "Then I might as well support you."

The three standing looked at each other with excitement, barely believing the Mayor's response.

The Mayor stood. "Will you please step outside, and give me a moment with my daughter?" He headed for the stairs.

Vincent rushed the others out. "Of course, Dad."

The Mayor looked back. "Let's stick to 'sir' for the time being, huh?"

Federico was confused and leaned over to Vincent as they approached the door and said, "I didn't know he was a knight." Vincent only smiled before closing the front door behind him.

The Mayor was left standing in the middle of the room. He looked up at the ceiling, towards his daughter.

Upstairs, Anna stood up from the floor where she had been desperately trying to hear every word. She understood enough to become unbearably excited. She looked to the locked door, to the window. She was a caged beast dying to be let out.

Elsewhere in the house, Gelsomina awoke with the dawn. She put on her typical Sunday clothes and headed for the bathroom to wash up.

Anna yet paced back and forth in her cage. She tried the door, but it was still locked. She called out the door, "Bambina!"

Bambina heard her amidst the loud swishing and cleaning of her teeth. "I'm busy!" she called back, muffled through the bubbles.

Anna finally returned to the window, noticing Vincent back outside, his eyes staring at her. She looked back at the locked door, and in doing so, noticed the tall roll of red carpet. She gathered it up in a flash, tossed the carpeting out the window to Vincent's waiting arms. Vincent spread the carpet out to make a slide. Anna placed both feet out the window before hearing the sound of a key entering the keyhole of her door. Her father burst in. She looked back at him with a smile. "Thank you, Dad." He smiled.

She jumped out the window, terrifying her father, who ran after her to the window. As he reached the window, he saw her sliding down to Vincent's arms. The momentum made them fall over, just in front of the door.

They kissed, Anna on top of Vincent, as half the City looked on from the lawn.

And suddenly, the front door whipped open, and Bambina appeared briefly to launch a can of paint up into the air, and down on top of the lovers. It never occurred to Vincent that this could perhaps be perceived as 'raining paint,' because he was a little preoccupied at the time. He would indeed think of it a few months later on a Tuesday.

Bambina had begun to shut the door again, but was startled by all the people in the lawn. She embarrassedly watched as the lovers embraced, soaked in her paint.

And so Vincent and Anna finally received the only success they had ever hoped for, yet they found that success at last, at last by discovering a secret so few in humanity ever discover: that success exists not in conquering, but in surrendering. The Mayor would someday see the success of his daughter's relationship too, the marriage of Vincent Fides and Anna Ratio, and he would see that his own surrender was the last stumbling block standing in their way.

A few hours later, Federico was speaking in the City Circle, flanked by Vincent Fides, the peddler of dreams, and Marie, his sister, whom the Mayor had pardoned instantly.

"The Corporation is finally in the hands of a man that will serve you, Artcity. But make no mistake about it. There are no endings or conclusions in human life- not even death can stop human power and ingenuity. My establishment as Ceo of the Corporation is not a happy ending at all, but only an acknowledgment of a new beginning, only a sign that a lot of work needs to be done. I will lead by serving you, Artcitizens, with all my heart and mind. I will establish a new relationship between the clowns and the City that we all love so well. This relationship will not be built on isolation or some false sense of tolerance. I don't want to be tolerated- I want to be respected.

"If tolerance means anyone can believe whatever they want, so long as they don't talk about it, then I won't accept tolerance. That view of tolerance has been detrimental to western civilization. But if tolerance means that we can all sit down at one long table and actually talk to each other, understand each other, as thinking, rational, civil men and women, then and only then, we are on the verge of a truly remarkable moment in history.

"And so I make this loud proclamation, calling for A New Dialogue of all humanity, that we might at last treat each other as a human family. We will disagree, and we will indeed argue, but only so long as it is built on a solid foundation of dignity, integrity, mutual respect, and a true love of humanity. This new world is not only possible, good people- it is inevitable. And we will march on toward this common goal either with you or despite you. So if you stand in our way, good enemy, beware- You are on the wrong side of history!

"But such an effort could only begin here in Artcity, friends. It cannot be accomplished by the petty politicians or the bumbling businessmen. Only the artists can lead us. We are the wayfarers of the old via pulchritudinis, the way of beauty. To be an artist is to hold precepts like integrity, honesty, goodness, beauty, and truth as close to our hearts as the blood that flows through them. Without these precepts, we will betray the very people who rely on us.

"We have seen many artists in the past reject these precepts altogether. They held in esteem not integrity but guile, not honesty but deception, not goodness but frivolity, not beauty but enticement, not truth but being fake enough to get fifteen minutes of fame. We have watched these artists lose the trust of their audiences, and watched as the world belittled us from artists into entertainers.

"We must rise up, Artcitizens, for the whole world needs us now more than ever before. Our New Evangelization begins now, dear friends. Let us fight for our lives. Let us give the world all the inspiration they could ever require, whether it's food for the pulpit, or drink for the tavern."

These tales of Artcity are already echoing throughout the continents, but little has been achieved quite yet. The revolution has been conceived- that's all. The revolution is growing, developing, maturing. Perhaps Vincent got his girl, but there is no real conclusion in a marriage, but rather, the door to a whole new set of battlefields. Should they fight together, perhaps someday they may realize that their happy ending happened long ago. But so is life, not in beginnings and endings, but in doors, and new opportunities to fight for what matters in life: Truth, and Providence. The people of Artcity succeeded because they stood up from their comfortable lives of routine and screamed one simple message. They screamed it from every rooftop and sound wave they could find. They stood up in a united voice and said, 'We will not be silent any longer.'

NOTES

Leave it to a Dominican to write a novel with annotations...

1. Chesterton, G.K. *The Victorian Age in Literature*. Chapter 2, The Great Victorian Novelists. New York: Henry Holt and Company, 1913.

2. A reference to the opening lines of Pope St. John Paul II's 1998 encyclical, *Fides et Ratio* ("Faith and Reason"): "Faith and reason are like two wings on which the human spirit rises to the contemplation of truth; and God has placed in the human heart a desire to know the truth—in a word, to know himself—so that, by knowing and loving God, men and women may also come to the fullness of truth about themselves."

3. A reference to the Angelus, which many Catholics pray every day at 6 a.m., noon, and 6 p.m. Many neighborhood churches still ring their bells at these times to signal everyone who can hear the bells to begin praying the Angelus.

4. Voltaire, Arouet de. Philosophical Dictionary. "Truth." New York: Carlton House.

5. Nietzsche, Friedrich. *Human, All Too Human: A Book for Free Spirits*. Part One: Miscellaneous Maxims and Opinions. Seventh Article. Translated by Paul Cohn. New York: The MacMillan Company, 1913.

6. Nietzsche, Friedrich. Human, *All Too Human: A Book for Free Spirits*. Part One: Miscellaneous Maxims and Opinions. Eighth Article. Translated by Paul Cohn. New York: The MacMillan Company, 1913.

7. A popular epigram of Friedrich Nietzsche describing his view of democracy.

8. A popular Aquinas quote that G.K. Chesterton used in his popular biography of St. Thomas Aquinas called *The Dumb Ox*.

9. St. Augustine is famous for this saying in the eighth book of *The Confessions*: "Give me chastity and continency, only not yet." The Project Gutenberg text is translated by Edward Bouverie Pusey.

10. From a popular Marian antiphon (or prayer) called, "Ave, Regina Caelorum," which is used from Candlemas through Wednesday of Holy Week in the Liturgy of the Hours and the Little Office of the Blessed Virgin Mary.

O Queen of Heav'n enthron'd,
Hail, by angels Mistress own'd
Root of Jesse, Gate of morn,
Of which the world's true light was born.
Glorious Virgin, joy to thee,
Lovliest whom in Heaven they see,
Fairest thou where all are fair!
Plead with Christ our sins to spare.

Ave, Regina caelorum,
Ave, Domina Angelorum:
Salve, radix, salve, porta,
Ex qua mundo lux est orta:
Gaude, Virgo gloriosa,
Super omnes speciosa,
Vale, o valde decora,
Et pro nobis Christum exora. Amen.

11. Pope Benedict XVI. Address to Artists. November 21, 2009.
12. Selections from the Song of Songs are sprinkled throughout Bambina's monologue.
13. Psalm 63: 1.
14. Second Book of St. Augustine's *Confessions*. Translated by Edward Bouverie Pusey.